A HOUSE CALLED MADRID

A House Called Madrid

R. T. PLUMB

DUCKWORTH

First published in 1980 by
Gerald Duckworth & Co. Ltd.
The Old Piano Factory
43 Gloucester Crescent, London NW1

© 1980 by R. T. Plumb

ISBN 0 7156 1484 3

British Library Cataloguing in Publication Data

Plumb, R T
    A house called Madrid.
    I. Title
    823'.9'1F   PR6066.L83H/

    ISBN 0-7156-1484-3

Typeset by Elanders Computer Assisted
Typesetting Systems, Inverness
and printed by
The Pitman Press, Bath

For
ROSEMARY HAWLEY JARMAN
with all of my love

1

Uncle Conway, for the first time in months, had been drunk all day. Or, more exactly, had been out all day getting drunk. Crouching just inside one of the rooms opening off from the hall, peering inquisitively out, I saw him arrive in the early evening. In his hands, as he staggered perilously, a long, unfamiliar box or case. His face, as he held the thing, was bellicose. His small eyes dishevelled as the rags our cleaning lady, Mrs Hampton, used. He was muttering to himself, trying to steer for the stairs, with the case, like a long unmanageable carcass, threatening to knock off his bowler or spiflicate his small double chins. Naturally it was easy for the small boy that I then was to follow without being seen, to creep up the stairs after him like a climbing spider. Uncle, bumping his way under a myriad dowdy dignified paintings, needed all his attention both to keep himself upright and the various pictures from being unhooked. The first landing, long and dark, echoed to his clumsy, scratching progress. Was he really trying to keep quiet? To smuggle something in? For that was what his furtive entrance, his darting eyes, had made me think.

In through the open door of a seldom used bedroom Uncle rocked, breath whistling, practically on his knees. While I hovered outside, moth-quiet on the landing carpet, he paused to catch his second wind, his head, under the seriously displaced bowler hat, wagging to and fro. At fifty Uncle Conway clearly found drink and exertion difficult to mix! Not like Aunt Wells who, although only a few years younger, could walk and walk, as well as climb the stairs in Dapperings emporium in town without the slightest faltering. A mirror set in the room's weightiest object — a large, ornate, dogeared wardrobe — showed his reflection to

7

unflattering perfection — shortish and pudgy, perspiring copiously inside a curled white wing collar, waxed eyebrows twitching
and shining. From time to time, as though punched, he discharged a soft, weary groan.

'Price for the boneyard, the blessed cemetery,' I heard him
mutter. 'If I can get him in his breeches!'

Still not understanding I jumped fearfully from the door as,
puffing, Uncle barged suddenly forward. But it was the wardrobe
he was charging at. Making considerable noise, Uncle crammed
his unwieldy burden deep among the scattering of old suits and
dresses. What was he hiding? Dare I ask? Flash went the
mirror-bright door, squealing on its hinges as Uncle tried to shut
it.

'Damn,' he breathed. 'The world's gone mad! Nothing's quiet
any more. Even wardrobes!'

Away I flew along the landing, down the stairs, along the
corridor, and into the large warm kitchen where Aunt Wells, at
work on a new recipe for home-made jam (utilising the last of the
winter's stored fruit) was tiredly wiping her fingers on a big,
equally tired, blue towel.

'Uncle's rolling,' I declared, enthusiastically. 'Like he did on
that boat at the seaside when I was little. Aunt Wells, he's been
drinking! I think he'll be sick!'

Aunt looked from me to the kitchen clock, its big moon face
encased in a judicial-looking, brown wooden frame. Half past six.
That was all. But Uncle Conway never had relied entirely on
public houses — when wildly thirsty, or depressed, he had flasks
to imbibe from.

Cutting short my babble — my theories on Uncle's mysterious
case seemed only to make her impatient — Aunt Wells moved out
and along to the ornament-cluttered hall.

'Conway, I want to see you,' she called up the stairs. 'And
please bring down whatever it is that you have just put in the guest
room wardrobe!'

From the landing above came a long, dreadful, wounded
silence. Turning, Aunt came back into the kitchen. Pushing aside
sticky spoons, jars, and sugar-curdled pots, she sat down at the
table. Her thin white forearms were faintly pebbled, her mouth
had a sudden downward chilly pucker, the apron that she always
wore for kitchen chores seemed suddenly capacious, leaving room
for her to shiver.

8

'Oh Gordon, after all this time. I thought, I really thought, that your Uncle had learnt his lesson. A drink, yes, even two or three, but — '

'He was rolling, Aunt Wells. Really rolling.'

All over again, as we sat waiting at the table, the erratic, lumbering noises — Uncle navigating the landing, descending the stairs, recuperation at the bottom, then the sound of his lurching down the passage.

Then, finally, in the kitchen, frowning, winking, swaying with uneasy pride.

'For — for our self-preservation, Wells, my rose. Though — though it was meant to be a secret.'

And, with an effort, grunting profligately, he laid the long strange case across the table, scattering, as he did so, Aunt's pots and jars.

Aunt Wells looked first at the case, and then at me.

'Time little boys with big, prying eyes, were in bed. Off you go, Gordon.'

Little! How dare she! Grimly, refusing to budge, I kept my gaze fixed on the hard grainy surface of Uncle's purchase.

'Bed, Gordon! With a prayer the instant you're inside your pyjamas.'

'I'm not little any more. Nine isn't little, nine and a quarter isn't little, nine and a half isn't little, and neither is ten little. And my pyjamas don't fit properly. There's a hole on the one knee already from saying too many daft long prayers!'

'My pyjamas — holes too,' Uncle said, grinning evilly, and swaying now with alarming abandon. 'Two for my feet, two for my arms, one for my neck, and one for — '

'Conway!'

'Sorry, Wells. Sorry, old heart.'

'Oh Aunt, be a sport,' I cried. 'Let me stay!'

'If you do not remove yourself this instant, Gordon — '

Outside the kitchen — after hurling shut the door — I remember lingering, ear pressed hungrily to the wood, knees bent ready for flight. The evenings were drawing out, and already sunlight was starting to penetrate the old town house, illuminating the stains on the faces of the ancient clocks, casting pale leaves of light on the dark carpets. But neither Uncle Conway nor Aunt Wells had brightness in their voices; it was beginning to sound

9

like one of their perpetual battles, with old, long established points of view brought out for yet another joust.

'Wells, dear old frog, we need a gun. Every — every household needs a gun. The oldest, most honourable form of defence in the world! Something a man can rely on if trouble brews, something a man can show to other men if — if they invade his property. Threaten his — his own little cabbage patch. God bless guns, I say, God bless 'em!'

'Conway! You know I detest anything of a military nature and yet, of all things, you bring — '

'It's covered, ain't it? Boxed. You can't see it. Hidden — hidden from your palsied eyes, ain't it?'

'You bring a gun into my house, and expect me not to mind! I don't care what it's hidden in. You can put it inside an Egyptian mummy for all I care, and I still won't have it. No gun, of any sort, is going to live inside my house. Even the sort they shoot at rabbits with.'

'Don't you talk pacifism to me,' Uncle shouted. 'We're besieged, woman, don't you understand? Besieged!'

'Anyone would think we lived in Spain, where the dreadful Civil War is. I think you are quite, quite mad!'

'Besieged, I say,' Uncle yelled, undeterred. 'That empty house, Belle Lilac, not fifty yards away, and likely, as sure as damn it, to be bought by that infidel. That — that Labour and Co-op! That's what he stood for our council as — Labour and Co-op. The cur! Thank God he failed! And now he wants to move among his betters, buy that big expensive house. Where has he got the money from, a chap like that?'

'Perhaps he has inherited a small fortune, as you did shortly after our marriage, Conway. In any case it is only rumoured that Mr Price is buying Belle Lilac. And, really, does it matter if he does?'

'We need a gun, damn it,' Uncle suddenly roared, voice foggy with defiance. 'Chap might call round for coffee! If he does, I want the seat of his pants stage centre!'

'Love thy neighbour,' Aunt Wells taunted, in a tone that meant she was exacting revenge — for after months of moderation on Uncle's part, this new roaring intoxication must have come all the more bitterly to her. 'Especially since I am sure that God's mercy extends even to Mr Price. Indeed, to all who wear that strange, misguided political label.'

10

'And what regard for our feelings did your late sweet neighbour at Belle Lilac have, selling to a cur like that? A damnation on Miss Young's palsied soul! I hope she sits and rots in her new home. I hope she sits collecting cobwebs, guilt and sorrow. The old faggot!'

'Miss Young,' flared Aunt Wells, 'as well you know, originally sold Belle Lilac to a *gentleman*.'

'Yes, and then the blighter went and died! Before he'd even moved in! And what does his widow do? Does she move in? Oh no! Returns it to the market. Sells it again.' Choking with rage, Uncle paused for breath. 'Now we look like having a — a Red there. Labour and Co-op! My God, talk about Armageddon! I tell you, Wells, I think it's a damn Red plot. The local Co-operative Wholesale Society taking over Belle Lilac. Well, why not? Funny that bloke should die before he'd even moved in. Funny his widow rushed to sell the place instead of moving in herself. Know what I think? I think Price — or the Co-op — murdered the poor blighter by arranging his heart attack, then paid the widow to sell. My God, talk about a Corsican secret society! It — it's plain what they want to do. Turn Belle Lilac into a Co-operative warehouse. Stuff it with their Cheddar cheese, tea packets, and damnably over-salted butter.'

'Oh Conway, really — '

'Corsican Secret Society!' Uncle thundered. 'CSS. Very like CWS, ain't it? My God!'

And then, his voice dipping low with a kind of crusty, fermented cunning, so that I immediately stooped to the keyhole: 'How did you know I'd got the damn shooter anyway? No one saw me enter, no one saw me go upstairs, no one saw me put it in the wardrobe.'

'Gordon saw you, Conway.'

'That boy,' Conway raged. 'He's my enemy, too. Why oh why did we ever consent to rear him? Why was he ever orphaned? Why — ',

A strange pause. Stooping afresh to the keyhole I saw Uncle bending over the table, cradling his stomach. Suddenly, braying out, he retched. There was a grating sound across the table. Aunt, forearms brisk as pistons, had pushed our large, flour-dappled pudding basin — recently used for a yellow cake with icing and dark fruit — under his small tumultuous mouth.

'Tomorrow, Conway,' Aunt said sternly, looking away, 'I shall return the gun, and any ammunition you may have foolishly bought. Defence and self-preservation against our future neighbour — if rumour is correct and Mr Price does become our neighbour — whatever next! Goodness knows I shall scarcely be able to sleep under the same roof as a shooting weapon. Oh there really ought to be a ban on guns. Or, better still, guns ought never to be made!'

Next morning, looking pinched about the eyes and a little less well tended than usual — rather like one of the carelessly assembled breakfast trays that Uncle Conway put together on her birthday — Aunt Wells came striding briskly through the hall carrying, in its case, the disputed gun. After a halt before a mirror, frowning at herself — at the mild, unfamiliar disarray — she put down the case and turned to frown at me.

'Gordon, why isn't your cap upon your head? You've had your breakfast, and I promised Mrs Taylor that you would spend the morning assisting her with various jobs.'

Saturday mornings assisting old Mrs Taylor, the corners of whose eyes were always full of fleece grey sleep! Ugh! But, if the gun could be kept, I'd never again grumble at having to visit her, or that small damp disagreeable house in the middle of an old cobbled alley.

'Oh, Aunt Wells, don't return it! Don't take the gun back!'

Aunt grew suddenly stiff. Quick stern dots moved inside her eyes.

'So you *were* listening last night. I suspected as much.'

'Why can't we keep it, Aunt Wells? I *like* guns!'

Aunt looked at me for a while, as if, after Uncle Conway, this was all a trifle hard to bear. Then, quite suddenly, she smiled, though not the kind of smile I should have trusted. It was too sweet, a little too full of her own singular brand of justice.

'After all, Gordon, I think perhaps we *should* keep the gun.' Then, as I grinned triumphantly, 'For one morning only! If I wait until this afternoon you can accompany me. Helping to carry it, and return it, should be a salutary lesson for you! Perhaps teach you not to meddle, perhaps instil a manliness that has nothing whatsoever to do with violence and firearms. Assuredly,' Aunt added, smiling her new sweet smile, 'assuredly I can possess my soul in patience for one short morning!'

2

It was by the river, actually overlooking the river, the place where Uncle had bought the gun, and to which Aunt Wells was so firmly whisking me, taking, as she did so, the opposite direction to town square, crossing tree-stitched roads and long green threads of traffic islands, past the corner field (cropped by an ageing horse called Dolly, to whom one gingerly offered acid drops) and down curving pearly roads. As she always did when heading for trouble she had walked as if part of the wind, her long stylish coat a flutter of light grey, her hat a conical affair of similarly shaded grey enlivened at the top by a crest of feathers. Yellow feathers, ruffled by the breeze. It was a springtime Aunt, trimmed for new conflicts, for an occasion of hard talking and no nonsense, for the salvoes only she could fire. Even if I was the one who carried the gun!

When she reached the building by the river she paused awhile, waiting for me to catch up with her.

'Do please hurry,' she called, adding, as I approached with dragging feet, 'One simply does not slow down at journey's end. To start briskly is of no merit unless one finishes briskly. You have been blown along on a breeze of exercise and exploration. Is that not so, Gordon? For that is the best description of a walk I know. Provided one has energy, and an inquiring mind, it is the only description.'

Ignoring this homily, I looked scornfully up at the tall sagging riverside building. Over the old decrepit green door — lurking at the top of rickety grey steps — a long rough plank had been slantingly riveted. Inscribed upon it, in faded green lettering, ran the words, 'A. Hall Mattey, Sporting and Other Requisites, Guns, etc.'

Aunt Wells, elongating her neck, looked quietly and determinedly upwards at this odd, leaning name-plank.

'Thank you, Gordon, you may now give me the gun case.'

'Aunt Wells — '

'The gun case, Gordon!'

Up the steps she went, holding the case with antipathy but safely clear of the apertures.

'Wait for me, Aunt Wells,' I called. 'I'm coming, too!'

After the brightness the sudden, swirling gloom. Odours, dusty and damp. Walls of dark, infinite height. Wickerwork baskets in square, pointing piles. Heaps of rolled canvas. All pressing down. And, away to the left, a long counter, the space behind it apparently empty — except for a long shelf. And that shelf, even in the gloom, bristling emphatically with what unquestionably was the shop's main business. Guns! Twisting and turning and leaning, as if surprised and curious at our entry, they paraded all along the shelf. Held roughly upright by two long stretches of parallel, light brown cord, they could have been the weaponry of a firing squad, bright arms at the slope! More guns than even Uncle Conway would have been prepared to buy!

'Look, Aunt Wells,' I breathed. 'Behind that counter. Guns!'

Aunt Wells was petrified. The gun case in her hand forgotten, she, too, was staring at the wall behind the counter. But not solely because of the guns! Pinned up in the middle of that row of rifles, was a big, white, damp-splotched text card!

'Beloved, let us love one another: for love is of God; and everyone that loveth is born of God, and knoweth God.'

I heard Aunt, breathless, murmur the text as if she had never before encountered it. My gaze, dropping, saw something move. Something humped and grey, shuffling just above the back edge of the counter.

'Aunt Wells, a ferret! A big stinking grey ferret!'

Up to the counter I rushed, hauling myself up, sprawling across its dusty width.

But no, no ferret! Up from the murky recess between counter and gun laden wall rose, instead, an only too human head of grey hair, and then, following in a kind of casual, stern unfolding, a tall, dusty looking gentleman!

'Lo,' said this gentleman, reaching out with cold long fingers to seize and pinch my collar, 'not a voice from heaven! Not the voice of angels! Not even the voice of angels crying, 'Ferrets, tally-ho!' Instead, a boy! A little Adam — though hardly old enough to wear a fig-leaf! Whatever next, I wonder, will the Good Lord send?'

14

Palpitating, still sprawled over the counter, up I gazed. Here was one of the most hairy gentlemen I'd ever seen. Hair seemed to assail him in huge, jutting waves. His head was a great grey wave, his eyebrows resembled splashed grey waves. A large compactly flowing moustache was like a grey rock awash with yellow foam. The eyes were chilling, a seaweed colour. And his lean neck, not too successfully shaven, glinted with tiny stiff grey hairs. Aunt Wells said later that he wasn't really old, only in his sixties! Amazingly, she also said he must once have been handsome. 'I can well imagine he brought the ducks off the pond in his younger days.'

'Ducks, Aunt Wells?'

'Young ladies, Gordon.'

Coughing from the tight clasp about my collar, I looked appealingly at Aunt Wells. She was smiling.

'This young boy does not appear to know the colour of a ferret. Or that someone looking for something in the shelves under the counter is hardly likely to be such a creature,' said the man, at last removing his cold long fingers. 'Mattey, Hall Mattey,' and, taking out a vast silver watch, he bowed gravely at Aunt Wells.

That was another thing about him. Not the bow, but the watch. Holding its face at a slightly tilted angle, he seemed curiously complete. A man of authority and wisdom, showing the world the importance, at any rate so far as he was concerned, of time.

'Gordon,' Aunt said, suddenly brisk again, 'remove yourself from that counter immediately. Disgraceful boy! Oh I do apologise, Mr Mattey. There are times when I altogether despair, and wonder if the old days, when boys existed on bread crusts and thin soup — if they were lucky — were not after all the best days for promoting health and good manners.'

'We live, alas, in an age of chewing gum. And Hollywood films,' said Mr Mattey, darkly. 'Of gangsters in short trousers. Dead-end kids, I believe they call them in America. The jazz babies, the razzle-dazzle offspring of the Twenties come home to roost! Infinitely sad, if I may say so. But we must strive. Strive and pray. The young are plants. The tender shoots that must be watered.'

Jazz babies! Aunt Wells may well have winced. Otherwise, Mr Mattey's oration was surely agreeable to her. It was resilient. It had been delivered with weight and dignity. It did not outlaw

15

hope. It spoke, with feeling, of the young. It was, in fact, a Christian statement, one dear to her own deepest sensibility. And, throwing back her head, yellow feathers nodding, Aunt Wells looked at Mr Mattey with both surprise and exultation —

'And now, madam — ' The watch was out again, its owner obviously impatient.

Recovering, Aunt became practical again.

'Very well, Mr Mattey. This gun. I believe that my husband bought it from you — '

And she moved forward, sliding the gun onto the counter, its case rumbling grittily along into Mr Mattey's chilly tapering hands.

The shop was cavernous. Leaving Aunt Wells now fully occupied, away I wandered, into its dusty depths. The dust, puffing off almost everything my elbows brushed, made nostrils curl, eyes water. On I poked, edging as though through an enemy encampment, with tent flaps and tent poles rising on all sides. Half-expecting, at any moment, those long lean fingers back behind my collar.

Suddenly, turning a corner past two tall clammy unexpected pillars of green and dun coloured linoleum, I came upon a tiny office.

Cautiously, I stepped inside. It was like stepping into a smudgy tumbler. The top half of the room was composed of murky glass on each of three sides. Dowdy old calendars and rusty, tin-plate advertisements for a biscuit called Munch littered the one solid wall. Cows, lowing from pit-dark fields, filled a tipsily hung oil painting. Next to it a large card, proclaiming, in stark black letters, God Speaks! And was that, under it, an actual picture of God? No, after scrutiny on tiptoe, I saw that it was merely a photograph of Mr Mattey.

Contemptuously, I turned to the square, rough hewn table in the office centre.

In a small cleared area between tawdry old cash books, clipped, browning invoices, and a pile of what looked suspiciously like text cards upside down — each in its turn awaiting resurrection? — was a penknife. Large and made of bone, it was open at the long blade end, and this exposed length of steel was moist with fresh red blood!

On that walk home beside the river — without the gun to worry her, Aunt Wells seemed to float along the towpath — I kept trying to tell her about the knife covered in blood, but either she wasn't interested or wouldn't listen.

'I simply could not get over it,' she kept saying.

'That text on the wall. God's word, flanked by rifles! It really was astonishing!'

Perhaps it was extraordinary — rather like getting a big white postcard from Jehovah. Receiving it, too, at a most opportune moment. Not that Aunt was superstitious, given to expecting messages or ecclesiastical straws in the wind — at no time could she have believed that God showed his face and will like a conjuror — but it had been a reminder that God is love, and everybody's neighbour. For welcoming Mr Price — if, that is, Mr Price did come to Belle Lilac — would not be easy. That terrible political complexion did make a difference. The prospect had appalled even Mrs Hampton.

'That Labour and Colic, lording it in that lovely big house,' she'd said, jabbing, with distaste, at dust on our banister. 'Shameful! I can't believe it will ever be allowed!'

But to Aunt's religiously imbued nature, all aversion, though felt, must now be conquered. Neighbourly niceties must and would be, observed. Mr and Mrs Price should not find her lacking, either totally, or in part, in the saving grace of human warmth.

'That text, Gordon, means only one thing. Love thy neighbour. There is no escaping that.'

I kicked a stone towards the river, watched it plop and vanish.

'Uncle Conway wants to shoot Mr Price. He said so!'

'Your Uncle, Gordon, is capable of the most outrageous bravado. He would, I admit, have liked to own a gun. An Englishman's indisputable right, and useful against burglars, or so he tried to argue. But that dreadful antique Cromwellian sword in the hall is quite enough for me. One dangerous weapon in a house is one too many.'

'Uncle says if he can't have the gun, he'll use the sword to shave off Mr Price's bum,' I said.

'Gordon, I will not approve that kind of talk! Aunt paused, looking speculatively down. 'And what, may I ask, put the idea of ferrets in your head? It was a most regrettable outburst.'

'Old Mrs Taylor said this morning she's got rats,' I said.

17

'She says she wants the ferrets in. She says ferrets climb walls and cling upside down, like limpets, to light bulbs. Then they drop down on top of the rats.'

'Oh dear,' said Aunt Wells as, borne by the breeze, we turned at last from the river. 'After next Saturday I think you really must cease helping Mrs Taylor. The poor woman's imagination is far too indulgent. No doubt she thinks that she knows how to entertain a young boy. But entertainment, without truth, is hollow and unedifying — harmful even.'

'I don't think it's imagination, Aunt Wells,' I said. 'I think it's the bottle of beer she drinks for breakfast! Or the grey sludge bunging up her eyes so that she can't see properly!'

3

Not all walks during that remote, hauntingly remembered late Thirties springtime, were with Aunt Wells. Uncle Conway, a writer of momentous political books that were either never completed or never started — for, certainly, they were never published — liked taking me the leafy, pleasant walk to the old Rialto. The huge white stucco wall, its bleakness coloured by posters, and enlivened by cabinets of still pictures from the films, emerged as one turned a corner by the church. Up the sweeping concrete steps, twinkling chubbily ahead of me, Uncle would bound. I think he would like to have taken me on Sunday evenings, emerging or entering just as Aunt was entering or emerging from church! He never did, though, and, on the whole, Aunt was tolerant of our excursions. All the same, she had doubts.

'I don't want Gordon unduly influenced by nonsense. There is so much nonsense in the world. Especially today.' And she would plaintively touch her dress, its high elegant front stately as a tablet over small constrained breasts, and turn her profile wistfully to the window. 'Not, though, that I am against an occasional treat.'

18

Treat? Such treats, for Aunt Wells, would have been mostly unendurable. For how was it possible to see a film without encountering, perhaps with painfully drawn out impact, that most recklessly dispensed of all Hollywood's benisons of the Thirties — the Last Kiss! A phenomenon usually presented in one of two ways — the knitting together, at the end of the last reel, of lips straining for a rosy future, or, if it were a sad film, the last kiss of lovers parting for ever. Aunt Wells, who had lost her first love at Ypres during the Great War, must have been terribly upset at such reminders. For her, too, there must have been, some-where, somehow, a last kiss, a last clasping in the arms of her soldier sweetheart.

Uncle, though, was unencumbered by such nostalgic humours. In the gloom of a seat in the stalls — squeaking, plum coloured plush beneath him — he really let rip. His throat would wear to a croak, his bow tie work loose, his small knees gib excitedly up and down. Only at news reel time did his mood change.

'Those damn Republicans,' he'd mutter, as film flickered on of the Civil War in Spain. 'We've got to wallop 'em. Send 'em flying! Beat the Mississippi mud out of 'em.'

'Isn't that in America, Uncle? The Mississippi?'

'Damn it, Gordon, I was only — Never mind!'

Looking up at the screen, at lines of bandaged soldiers shamb-ling along with their hands lifted in surrender, 'What are they fighting for, Uncle Conway?' I asked. 'Why are they killing and capturing each other?'

'Double damn it, Gordon, I've told you a thousand times! Something had to be done. The Spanish Parliament was rotten to the core.'

If Uncle could talk intelligently, so could I! 'Rather like those bad apples Aunt Wells threw away last summer. The ones with maggots and brown centres in them?'

'If you like. Those who cherish law and order couldn't possibly support that Parliament, or the Republican government. So, rather than submit, some of the Spanish generals have launched a revolution.'

'Revolution, Uncle Conway? You said the other day that the revolution was wicked. Mad, bad dogs let loose, you said. I heard you.'

Uncle writhed in his seat.

'That was the Russian revolution, Gordon. The Bolshevik

19

blood bath! The Spanish revolution is different. The Nationalists, led by General Franco, fighting the government.'

'What's wrong with the government?'

'Weak, Gordon, weak. Only too ready to pander to the Reds.'

'Was the bad apple Parliament full of Reds?'

'Yes, my boy, exactly. Put there by so-called workers! Syphilitic, idle peasants, more like! The whole damn Parliament and country run by Reds and Socks!'

Socks! Uncle's latest sobriquet for Socialists. And, to me, a strange indelible intertwining — Socks and the Spanish war! Such a homely word. Even I wore socks! What kind of socks did the Reds wear? Well, red surely. And the others? So long as soldiers on either side marched to their war in differently fashioned, differently hued, hosiery, all would be well, I felt. Unthinkable that men shooting to kill each other should wear the same colour! Oh yes, and perhaps the Reds — for I had a feeling it might be so — wore well darned socks. Socks clumsy with thick unfriendly repair wool that tried to keep sore, tramping feet respectable. As I watched those old news reels, with their lines of captured Republican troops for ever on the screen, something stirred in me.

'It's not fair, Uncle Conway. Those prisoners! Bet they've holes in their socks! Nasty big holes. Big enough to let the blood out!'

Sometimes, too riveted by the pictures on the screen to answer questions, Uncle seemed to shrink morosely in his seat, his hands clasped over crumpled waistcoat, short curled up leg sticking out into the gangway, his shoe ghostily reflecting yet another aspect of that Spanish war — guns bursting, unshaven soldiers running for cover, and all finishing up as no more than flickers and eddies of light on the end of polished leather! What a way for a day of serious war to end, as little more than a shimmer on the tip of Uncle's laces! But such profundities were then hardly mine. The only incongruity I ever perceived was when Uncle, after coughing his way through one Craven A, immediately lit another.

The Saturday following the visit to the gun shop by the river, I met Uncle Conway in the street. I think that he had been drinking at the Bear and Old Brunswick. He looked a shade pink in the face, and when he saw me he raised his bowler hat!

'Aren't you coming home to dinner, Uncle?' I said. 'There's ham and swedes, with butter sticking up and plenty of salt and pepper.'

'Swedes, boy! Swedes! Damn great watery orange cow pat of a vegetable if ever there was one. Still — ' and, jovially enough, he tapped his stomach.

Together, Uncle's hand clamped on my shoulder, we crossed the road. We crossed obliquely, passing the corner on which stood the York Arms, Uncle's favourite hostelry. (Until he had been asked, by the landlady, to stay away!)

'God alive!' Uncle said, stopping, on wobbly legs, to stare. 'My sainted aunt in Jamaica!'

What was wrong? All seemed in order. The little forecourt, sloping gently up from the pavement. The crooked front steps. The long bow window of the bar. And, higher up, the plain faced, sloping bedroom windows.

The only new object, standing between two cellar gratings — about as long as the bow window immediately above it — was a freshly installed, freshly painted, bench!

'Horrible,' Uncle fumed, under his bowler a suddenly richer pink. 'Did you ever see a more ghastly colour?'

The bench was a bright red.

'What taste! But then, she never did have any judgment!'

Suddenly I felt an eerie chill. Quickly I glanced up at the bedroom windows. Was *she* up there, watching? Mrs Hallet? The weird widowed lady who ran the Arms, and who wore a black beauty spot in the centre of her brow?

'I haven't seen Auntie Alex for such a long time, Uncle Conway,' I said. 'Is she dead? Or up there watching us?'

'Damn it boy, Mrs Hallet to you. She's no more your aunt than the man in the moon!'

She didn't look like the moon either, I thought — except perhaps for breasts like full, pale globes. On one memorable occasion I had seen them in their unmoored, quivering entirety by accidentally invading her bedroom. Though only partially nude she had screamed and screamed! That, though, wasn't why Uncle had been asked to stay away. He had been asked to stay away because of his rantings and generally impossible behaviour. That he had previously been to Blackpool on a furtive holiday with Auntie Alex, when he should have been elsewhere research-ing for a book, hadn't helped him either — it seemed that he had

21

ranted and been generally impossible at Blackpool too! Saddest of all though, Aunt Wells had found out about that surreptitious holiday!

And, remembering, something of last summer's pain came back, Aunt's unhappiness, her sudden departure from home, and then her return and apparent peace with Conway. But although, so far as I knew, they never spoke of Auntie Alex, I think she may have been often in their minds.

'Did you kiss her in Blackpool when you went there with her, Uncle Conway?' I asked, squinting up at the round pink face under the bowler.

And I thought how it would be to kiss that strange, self-styled auntie, rubbing one's lips deep into that dauntingly rouge and powder caked cheek, smelling gin or sherry on breath that glazed the air! — peeping into scooped out necklines while one stood on tip toe — clutching, perhaps, her big pale thumb to keep balance! For once, when we'd met in the park, she actually had talked about kissing, saying that in the days when she courted her dear late Noel Hallet, he had sat with her on a grave and put his tongue into her mouth. No doubt that's what she'd want me to do, and perhaps what Uncle Conway had already done, and didn't it sound awful! Sitting amid tombstones sticking tongues into mouths. Ugh! And I bet she'd want me to put my tongue into her mouth right over her husband's grave! *What would it be like,* that contact? Slimy and horrible? Like licking the dead fish that Aunt Wells had left in the kitchen on a plate, and that I had licked from curiosity because its silvery shine had seemed to beg caress? Or would it be unimaginably different from anything experienced before? One thing I was sure of, and that was how her voice would sound. Swampy, ingratiating as her dense black eyelashes, saying in my ear, 'Always looking for a new gentleman, a new Noel, that's me. 1922 when my Hallet died, and still my prince ain't come. How about you for my hub, eh, little man?'

It was all too easy, in my sudden, squirming distaste, to forget that, last summer, I'd been in love. With Auntie Alex's beautiful, grown-up daughter! Betty, I mournfully knew, had left the Arms to marry a little piano tuner called Mr Edgar. So long ago since last I saw them! As if swept away with the dried brown leaves of autumn, they seemed gone for ever.

'Damn you, boy, did you hear me?'

I looked up. Bowler hat tipping, Uncle Conway was glaring down.

'Don't mention Mrs Hallet, or Blackpool, to your Aunt! Do you understand me, Gordon? She can do without being reminded of that insalubrious vulgar watering-place. As for Mrs Hallet — '

And, abruptly silencing himself — as though he'd already said too much — Uncle Conway turned unsteadily away.

Our house, near the square, had only just been reached when, dramatically, from behind one of the tall, lightly waving trees in the drive, Sam appeared. Weathered and grubby as an old vegetable root, he looked as if he had been booted straight from some furrow in the earth — propelling and rotating himself towards us. The high, corduroyed rump that simply refused to tuck itself decently away, came with him — hobbling, as it were, in the rear.

'Almighty heavens,' Uncle groaned. 'Not that grumbling crate of bone and bum! One of these days we'll get ourselves a real gardener. God, and Wells, willing.'

'Looks like rain,' Sam gasped, puffing past us and forgetting, in his turbulence, to throw at Uncle his usual look of scorn. 'Too late to wet the new 'un at Belle Liluc, though. The bugger's in! The furniture van's been a-emptying there all morning.'

'Oh God,' said Uncle Conway, his rotund body suddenly very still. 'Oh God! Armageddon!'

Leaving Uncle, I moved away between the trees, treading through old raspberry canes and thickets of winter stunted growth that should, by rights, have long been cleared. As the undergrowth grew more dense I had to hop and twist — but not for long. The wall stopped me, the wall that, for part of its length, we shared with Belle Lilac. An old secretive moss tufted structure of ripe yellow brick, it looked exactly, disappointingly, as it always had.

23

4

Next day, Sunday, brought an evening of mystery. Aunt Wells, promptly retiring after tea to her bedroom, proceeded to intrigue me. Through the closed door I heard an occasional rustle as dresses, taken from the wardrobe, slid and slopped like captive, dying fish, all over the large, immaculate bed. In my mind's eye I could see them all spread out, each quite exquisite. Which would it be? The dress she called her Hanging Gardens of Babylon dress, because of its discreet falls and folds? The Red Sea Parting dress — a surge of colour at the throat, a clotted pink estuary high above a long cream sea? Or the blue dress known as the Lake of Galilee? Unusual for so much hesitation! And was that scent I smelt? The merest whiff, of course. Utterly ladylike, but still delightful. What was she doing now? If only keyholes were bigger! My eye, pressed to this particular keyhole, presently encountered a steady blur of blue. Aunt, it seemed, had at last made her choice! Eye watering, unable to stand any more draught, I drifted reluctantly to Uncle's study. Here blue also predominated as Uncle, sitting behind his desk, joylessly puffed a cigar. The news about Belle Lilac had plummeted him to the depths; he had become as cramped and gloomy as the smallest, darkest of our rooms. Even Aunt's excellent lunch — for once, strangely, she hadn't gone to the eleven o'clock morning service at the church up the avenue — had failed to tempt that small, usually eager mouth. A kind of revenge, perhaps, for Aunt taking the same news so lightly? Sulky rejection of roast beef and horse-radish sauce to prove his bitterness? As for Aunt receiving the news so equably, that was only to be expected. All the same, I thought, she appeared to be finding life almost *too* lovely on this particular Sunday. Was something else on her mind? And if so, what? Why no church that morning? Why had she been wearing a small pleased smile, and practically swirling on air through rooms and passages? Why had I caught her continually humming her favourite hymn? And now, in her

24

room, dressing up and taking simply ages! Glumly I looked at the clock on Uncle's desk. Only half past five. The venetian blinds were up, the garden outside coldly sunning itself beyond the trees of the drive.

'Aunt seems different, Uncle,' I said. 'Like a soap bubble. Is she going to burst?'

Uncle, podgy legs up on his desk, was evidently waiting for Aunt to depart for church. After which, lighting a fresh cigar, he would either depart for the Bear and Old Brunswick, leaving me alone, or, with a flask or bottle, entrench himself even more firmly in the study. If he went, what then? The house held no more secrets. Nor did I really enjoy the lonely feeling as night came on, the garden retreating from the house into a chill hazy independence, the house folding itself darkly against the garden. Even the companionable muttering of the tall old clocks along the corridor becoming cold, remote.

Suddenly, on the lazy evening air, I heard a chugging! The swelling, shaking sound of a rough old engine. A car! In our drive! Chug, chug, chug! Chug, chugga, chug!

Rushing eagerly to the window, I saw a most elderly looking car — square and black, with big brassy headlamps. Bumping to a halt under the trees it stood for several minutes quaking and rattling, before, with a final bump and quake, becoming quiet and still.

'Uncle, a car! A strange motor car!'

Whipping down his legs Uncle came quickly to the window.

'Who the devil,' he asked grumpily, 'can it be?'

We watched, holding our breaths. A tall, elderly man, his fading Homburg hat sitting like a large grey duck on a rampant crest of thick grey hair, got out of the car. Taking out a silver pocket watch of obvious dignity, he looked carefully and expectantly towards our porch.

'Why, it's Hall Mattey, the gun dealer! Or whatever he calls himself,' Uncle said. Flabbergasted, he put his cigar back between his teeth.

'Yes,' I said excitedly. 'Aunt took me to see him. He has cold hands. And a knife all covered with blood!'

Without answering Uncle turned and, followed by me, went quickly to Aunt's bedroom. Pausing outside he hesitated, then instead of knocking or opening, called testily through.

'Wells, that damn gun merchant from beside the river's just driven up. Do you know what he wants?'

'Oh dear,' I heard Aunt say. 'He's early! Please tell him that I'll be down shortly.'

Baffled, Uncle gazed at the door. Then, shrugging, 'We'd better descend, lad,' he muttered. 'See what it's all about.'

There had been no knocking, or ringing of the bell, and when Uncle opened the front door Mr Mattey was still near his car, under the majestic line of old trees.

'Oh good evening,' he called, on seeing us.

As he paced lankly across the drive towards the porch, clutching his watch, he seemed more than ever a man splashed by grey hair.

'Trees!' he said, reaching the porch and thrusting out a long, cold looking hand for Uncle to shake. 'What a sight they always are! Especially in a driveway. The tallest, most gracious of decorative entities, I always think. Mattey, Hall Mattey. You remember me, of course. That gun you bought—'

'Er, yes,' Uncle mumbled, flushing.

'And our young hob ferret, I see. Splendid, splendid. Hallo, young Adam.'

'Hallo,' I muttered.

There ensued a most uneasy silence. With Uncle waiting stiffly for an explanation.

'The text card!' said Mr Mattey, abruptly. 'That's what began it. That's what got your wife and I talking.'

Text card?

Uncle, gripped by a sudden, pagan aversion, glowered at the buttons on Mr Mattey's jacket.

Mr Mattey, caressing his watch, looked thoughtfully down at Uncle. Then, finally realising that Uncle had no intention of speaking first, 'But perhaps, sir, you didn't notice? When you were in my shop, I mean. Though not everyone will admit to noticing the word of God, even when they do!'

'I noticed nothing,' Uncle muttered. 'Text card, you say. Where was the thing?'

'Where, sir? Why, on my shop wall. Behind the counter. A counter, may I add, where ferrets lurk.' And, winking, Mr Mattey looked at me.

Uncle, now completely baffled, gave a tiny, enraged shuffle of shining black shoes.

26

'As I was saying, not everyone will admit to noticing God's word. But they do, oh yes. That's why, most days, I change the card. Put up a fresh text. To help, maybe, some customer with trouble on his soul.' Mr Mattey paused, then, sailing blithely on, 'Indeed, some days are extraordinary. *His* days. I wake up. Hear Him whispering. As if I were Samuel's ear. Know that I must do my duty. Change the card. And, by so doing, change, perhaps, the direction, the destination, of someone's life. That, sir, is living. Discharging, however, humbly, the divine will!'

And, with a satisfied nod of grey head and fading Homburg, Mr Mattey tucked away his watch.

'That's like bus drivers and bus conductors,' I said, scornfully. 'They change the names of places on their buses all the time. So that people can see where the buses are going. They wind big rolls up and down. Then sometimes they take one down and put up another roll. Haven't you seen them? Uncle Conway has, haven't you, Uncle Conway?'

Suddenly Uncle Conway wasn't listening. He was staring over my head. A lady in a black hat, a single scarlet cherry pinioned to the wide, floppy brim, had stepped from the black car, banging the door behind her.

'Ah,' said Mr Mattey, taking his bemused, seaweed coloured eyes from mine, and looking round, 'my daughter, Charlotte!'

'Good evening,' Uncle Conway called, stepping gallantly from the porch. At that moment, looking radiant, Aunt Wells came from the hall behind us. Her lightweight springtime coat deliberately unbuttoned at the top to show the limpid blue of her dress of Galilee. Under a tall white hat of absolute simplicity, her cheeks pink, her eyes aglow.

Uncle, with a quick, regretful look across the drive, stayed where he was.

'Mr Mattey,' said Aunt Wells, turning quickly to Uncle, 'is a trustee of a little mission hall in the country. He has kindly invited me to a service there. Is that not so, Mr Mattey?'

'Indeed yes, dear madam. For, Stretch out thy hand, saith the Lord to his servant, and all shall be possible. Lo, even the daughters of the Church of England shall come breathless to thy fold. Clad in raiment of blue and white, to gladden the eye, and warm the heart. Grace be theirs. They shall be made welcome, even in the most humble of my abodes.' And Mr Mattey closed

27

his eyes, turning lean palms outwards like a Pope about to bless.

Aunt, instead of being overwhelmed, looked touched and amused. Uncle Conway, eyes bulging, stood rooted.

'We shall not be late back, shall we, Mr Mattey?' Aunt cried anxiously. 'That wouldn't do at all.'

'We shall not be late back,' said Mr Mattey. Somewhere deep in the peculiar eyes I thought I saw a sudden, tiny twinkle. 'Have faith in Daniel Damascus.'

'Daniel Damascus?' Aunt's eyebrows rose.

'My car! My old jalopy. A whim of mine, dear madam. The day after I moved, like Saint Paul, into light. Should my most cherished possession, my oldest pal, be left unnamed — a heathen — while I moved on?'

Aunt, smiling again, looked at Uncle Conway to see if he was smiling. He wasn't.

'Aunt Wells,' I remarked, for something to say, 'is wearing one of her christened dresses. Her Lake of Galilee dress. The dress that makes Uncle Conway shout!'

And I thought of the day when the Lake of Galilee dress was brand new from the shop. Aunt, wearing it for the first time at home, was showing it to Uncle.

'Isn't it the most fascinating blue? The blue of the water, and skies, in those old days in the Holy Land, around Galilee. At least, that's what I thought when choosing it in Dapperings. And I shall call it just that. My Lake of Galilee dress!'

And Uncle Conway's inevitable riposte (for how could he ignore such provocation).

'Wear it then. No doubt you'll be able to walk on the water in it! Rise over the waves like — like blue yeast!'

And Aunt, flushing, suddenly in armour for her faith.

'Oh really, Conway, must you? Even if you don't believe, you could at least show tolerance.'

'Tolerance? Oh take your walk on the water. Fall in and drown yourself!'

'Wrong! I shall never never drown! I shall be invisible, part of that marvellous lake! Blue in blue! For, if you are part of the water, at one with its clear and lapping beauty, how can you drown?' Then, after a pause, swallowing, 'Conway, the hooks at the back. Please? I can't quite — '

'Call on your Saviour to help you. I haven't His miracle-working hands!'

And Aunt, suddenly bitter herself, clasping hands over her breasts as if they were not her hands but those of some longed for lover.

'You're right, Conway. You haven't!'

'Lake of Galilee dress?' said Mr Mattey now. 'I am not alone, then, in biblical christenings?' From under his matted eyebrows he looked, rather curiously, at Uncle Conway. 'But, sir, how could a mere dress make you shout? If, indeed, you did!'

'At times,' said Aunt Wells, blushing, 'Gordon likes to draw attention to himself. Don't be ridiculous, Gordon.'

'The boy's mad,' Uncle growled. 'Needs a thrashing.'

'But you did shout, Uncle Conway. The dress made you shout. I heard!'

There was a long pause. Mr Mattey, as if cogitating upon my madness, stood staring at me.

'Baskets!' he said dramatically, apparently plucking the word out of the air without rhyme or reason. 'Yes, baskets. That humble, vital, everyday commodity. I never see a boy, any boy, but what I think of baskets!'

Was he barmy? Why, horrors, he was actually kneeling down to talk to me. So close to my own face that I could clearly see those pale yellow streaks in his sea-washed, granite moustache. It was like looking at the faded yellow checks in one of Uncle's old sports jackets! His breath, too, enigmatic and old — like the inside of a wardrobe!

'You must know the story,' Mr Mattey said, peering into my eyes. 'The feeding of the multitude. The five thousand. And the lad with the basket of five barley loaves and two fishes.'

'I haven't any loaves and fishes,' I flared, horribly embarrassed. 'And I hate baskets! Aunt Wells sometimes makes me carry them.'

Mr Mattey was undeterred. His eyes, and breath, stayed formidably close.

'I imagine you like barley sugar sweets though. Eh, young Adam? All boys do.'

This was better. Out, tentatively, went my hand, palm upwards.

But Mr Mattey only shook his head. 'No, I haven't any. Have you?'

I shook my head.

'Then there is nothing for us to multiply. Is there, boy? No start can be made on nothing.'

Full of hatred, gritting my teeth, I remained silent.

'Each boy born on this earth, like that boy of long ago,' went on Mr Mattey, looking at me hard with his beach algae eyes, 'is a bundle of possibilities. Possibilities for good. Possibilities for evil. Like the lad with the basket. God took what that fledgeling had to offer, and multiplied it richly. But, alas, my boy, what have you to offer?'

I heard Uncle Conway shuffle his feet and thought he groaned. Aunt Wells, I saw, was looking rather happier. But the sermon wasn't over.

'Take Charlotte,' said Mr Mattey.

We looked towards the car where — her wide brimmed hat slightly swaying like the branches above her — Mr Mattey's daughter stood impatiently waiting.

'There, hob ferret, is an example! when she was little, no older than you, we gave her her own plot of land. In which to grow produce. In which to multiply the good seed. And she did! She grew the most striking, most gratifying cabbages for miles. Little Queen Cabbage! that was what we called her.'

Little Queen Cabbage! Shrinking with horror, I glanced up at Uncle Conway. A sloppy look on his face, he was once more gazing at the lady by the car.

'So, remember. A bundle of possibilities. That's each young boy,' and, with just a flick of cold finger against my nose, Mr Mattey creaked to his feet.

'Come, dear madam. Daniel awaits!'

After being cranked and turned, no easy task, off, suddenly, the black car went, bucking fierily down the drive.

'Well, I'm damned,' said Uncle Conway, sitting down in the porch and staring after the car. Wells might have told him! Blast her religiosity! Probably the chap was fawning after their money for his wretched country chapel! Devil take it, a man who, when he wasn't selling guns, was Jesus creeping! And, huffily, Uncle Conway sat there in the porch, staring down the drive until the sound of Daniel Damascus was no more than the merest rattle in the breeze.

30

5

The magazine lay open on Uncle Conway's desk. It had been there half the winter, always open at the same pages. Uncle, fascinated, filled every idle moment with yet another perusal. 'It's about the Civil War in Spain,' he told me, over and over again. Illustrating the article were two photographs. One of these, taking a whole page, showed an exceedingly handsome gentleman with thick eyebrows, a good nose, and — directly under the proud nostrils — a rather narrow, tall moustache. Over an army uniform was slung a cape or coat with a fur collar. Around the middle of this military man was a dark sash. This, as Uncle explained, was Caudillo, Generalissimo Francisco Franco! rising star of Spanish Fascism, protegé of Hitler and Mussolini and scourge of all Republican loyalists. It must have been a picture that gave Uncle much pleasure. Perhaps he saw something of himself, for here, surely, behind the dignity, was a man with inner political fire. The picture on the other page showed a lorry on a dusty rocky road. The lorry crammed with soldiers waving and grinning. The sky behind them lonely and ungraven except for one or two straggles of cloud or gun smoke. In the foreground a low crumbling stone wall with an old black-shawled peasant lady sitting on it, hands clinging to her basket as though it were the centre of her world. The lorry itself, a tumbledown vehicle, was somehow the most predatory part of that bleak rough landscape, making one feel that it, at any rate, would burp and grind forever onwards.

'Nationalist troops on the move,' Uncle said at last, rapping with down turned knuckles the glossy page before him. 'Reinforcements for besieging Madrid, I shouldn't wonder. Franco's men. And, by God, a health to 'em!' And Uncle, after a great swig from his flask, drove his thumb squarely down into the middle of the Spanish lorry. As though shattering, for all time, that cheerful roadside moment of respite. Of peace from the shell-whistling winds of war. As though forever to imbue lorry and soldiers with his own spirit, his own will. Proceed and conquer, that twisting, pressed down thumb appeared to say. Roll on! The world is yours!

The half hour since Aunt's departure for the country in Mr Mattey's car had been long and irascible. Uncle, still chafing at the indignity of it all, had retired to his study taking me with him. But having arrived at the study and taken out his flask, he had begun to churn away about Spain like an old stuck gramophone needle! Mr Flood, my teacher at school, had told us once that, in Spain, everyone prayed. It was a religious country. You wouldn't have thought so to hear Uncle! According to Uncle, some sort of crusade was going on aimed at destroying a Red Christ. Long live the Red Christ, for He is one of us! That, Uncle spluttered indignantly from under his dipping flask, was how the workers talked in Spain. Never mind that the Church was supporting Franco! What about the Church's master? What about this Red Christ, then? Who was He supporting? Not Franco, that was sure. And then had come the long silence with Uncle staring at the picture of the lorry —

'Fighting for us, Gordon, that's what they're doing!' Prodding, for the second time, the unfortunate soldiers. 'Hammering the Red Christ! Fighting to remove the corrupt Madrid government. While here, in England, your Aunt gets her head stuffed with love-your-neighbour nonsense!'

It was time, I thought, to change the subject.

'Silly old Queen Cabbage!' I said, abruptly. 'Barmy old flop hat.'

'Eh?'

'That lady by the car,' I said. 'Wasn't she silly? Wearing a cherry. I bet if I ate it I'd get gut ache.'

'That's enough, Gordon. I've told you before, I won't have coarseness.' Frowning, Uncle took another tremendous, gurgling swig. 'Nor disrespect. The lady looked charming.'

'But she *was* silly. And only dafties grow cabbages!'

'There are times, boy, when you get on my nerves.'

Testy again, Uncle slapped shut the pages of his magazine — it was to be hoped that Franco's noble face did not slap down too hard on the lorry load of his own soldiers as they smiled from the opposite page! — pulled to his feet, belched aggrievedly, and trotted like a suddenly restive pony to the window. The venetian blinds were down. Clicking them apart he peered through.

'What is Aunt Wells' head stuffed with the Bible for, Uncle Conway?' I asked. 'You said that it was stuffed with love ... love your neighbour, or something. Isn't that in the Bible? She doesn't actually eat the Bible, does she?'

And I imagined, with a deep, unholy joy, my fastidious Aunt cramming her refined mouth with the gilt-edged pages of Deuteronomy, Leviticus and Ezekiel.

'God alive, Gordon, your sense of humour!' I heard Uncle mutter from the region of the blinds.

'You said that her head was stuffed, Uncle Conway. You did!'

'I think, after all, a visit to the Bear and Old Brunswick,' Uncle barked, looking almost fevered as he turned to face me. 'Which means, Gordon, that you're placed on trust. In other words, do what you like, but be in bed before your Aunt gets home. And don't leave the house. Understood?'

It was useless, I knew, to ask to accompany him. Already, like the Spanish sky in the photograph, the house was changing to the lonely, empty feeling I knew so well.

'Yes, Uncle Conway,' I said wearily.

Belle Lilac, as seen from its front gate — a charming little picket-fence of a gate, with the house name, in blue, clinging patchily to a rugged, erratically tacked strip of wood — was the only view of the property that I knew. This was because the late owners, Miss Cuthbert and Miss Young — Miss Cuthbert now gone to heaven, Miss Young to Birmingham, from where came an occasional letter smelling of lavender and addressed to Aunt — had not particularly liked, or encouraged, boys. Oh Aunt Wells had visited them. On special occasions — such as a birthday — for cake and port, though Aunt, no drinker, endured rather than enjoyed what Uncle bellicosely referred to as: 'Port wine and madeira cake! Not drinking at all. Just a damned ceremony for the squeamish.' On no occasion had Aunt taken me or Uncle Conway. It would have been like putting vipers into a cage of canaries, for I vividly remembered the two ladies, clad in their favourite yellowy green tweeds, with soft blue scarves tucked about their ageing necks, fluttering and gasping over their little front gate whenever — my tongue defiantly out — I strutted by. When — in conversation with Aunt Wells — I had learnt that angora wool came from rabbits, and that the scarves the ladies wore were angora, and that they kept hutches full of angora rabbits somewhere in their back garden, I had been strangely angry.

'Bunny pluckers!' I'd yelled down their path (at the time they were flapping and quivering over an ants' nest, Miss Cuthbert's hands — like two pale birds learning to fly — twittering outwards and upwards in the air). 'Rotten barmy bunny pluckers! Yah, yah, yah!'

Now, standing at their once sacred gate in the mildewy quiet of the bright but fading Sunday evening, I looked anew at the same old vista. To left and right a screen of tall trees. From the gate, leading straightly to Belle Lilac, a longish path, bleak oblongs of vegetable garden on either side — Miss Cuthbert and Miss Young had been as proud of growing their own produce as of making their own scarves. Belle Lilac itself belied its fragrant name. A long, flat house with a reluctant porch and large square windows that disliked the sun. And, just now, with the unfriendly look of a piano with the lid shut. Yet, inside, somewhere in the forbidding gloom of unknown rooms and passages, was our new neighbour, the terrible Mr Price. Terrible, at least, to Uncle. Aunt Wells hadn't seemed to mind quite so much. And, cautiously, I opened the gate — the strip of rough wood with the blue painted name catching at my trousers — and stepped through. Moving quickly behind the nearest tree, I duly considered. A dash to the house, exploring round the side and rear for the old rabbit hutches that must surely still be there? A peep through a window to catch a glimpse of Mr Price? Why not?

Gripping Uncle's magazine, a rolled glossy cudgel in my hands — after Uncle had gone I'd picked it up from the desk to swipe at a sunbeam and hadn't put it down again — out from behind the trees I sprang. As I ran, the ghosts of Miss Cuthbert and Miss Young, one from heaven, the other from Birmingham, must have blanched and turned to steaming mist! For, neglecting the path, I hared low to the earth all down the middle of one of the long vegetable patches — not that there was anything to see in the way of vegetables, only weeds — reaching, with a final, triumphant, side-stitching burst, the thin line of bushes just before the big, mysterious house!

From the bushes I stared at the windows. No movement. Only static gloom and dark green, sloppily drawn curtains. Everything wrapped in a grim Sunday seclusion. Yet, would the ladies, at any second, peer tremulously out? It still didn't seem real to me that Miss Cuthbert had been put into a coffin — placed carefully in as I'd once placed, in a box, a dead, sad starling — and that Miss Young had left to live elsewhere. Only what I remembered seemed real, Miss Cuthbert and Miss Young flitting with sparrow energy up and down their path, scarves like pretty rumpled banners at their fragile throats. And now? Mr Price? Could somebody of that name really be living here, in their house?

Out from the bushes and up to the porch I went. Bold as an errand boy, I stared up at the front door. Suddenly, lifting the rolled-up magazine, I forced it half through the brassy, retreating flap of the letter box. An impromptu megaphone. One of those things people shouted into!

'Up the Socks!' I thundered, lips frothing at the round mouth of the paper. 'Hurrah for the Labour and Co-op! Hurrah for the Red Christ!'

And then, like one of the angora rabbits I'd never seen, away I hopped, low under the windows, round to the darker, damper side of the house. There, between the brickwork and a giant bush, I waited. Each beat of my heart frighteningly loud. Opposite was a wall, its bricks the colour of putrefying fruit. *Our* wall too, I thought suddenly. On the other side, our garden! If only it weren't so tall. If only I could climb it! Then, as quiet persisted and confidence returned, I began, daringly, to edge further along the side of the house.

At the end I paused, peering round the corner. The garden at the rear was quite rank. An empty birdbath, black and cracking. Old derelict trees and drooping weeds. A conglomeration of wire and wood that could have been old hutches. A shed peppered by rusty nails. Splitting flower tubs.

Suddenly the sun went. Everywhere chill. Particularly so, perhaps, here at Belle Lilac's rear. Shivering, I stepped out from the corner of the wall. To my surprise, the back of the house was not like its front, perfectly straight all across its width. The wall went only a short way, stopping at a tall dark window, then moving outwards at right angles before, presumably, again running parallel with the front.

That window was irresistable. Along I crept to the stone crust of sill — it came as low as my knees — and then in I peered. At first I saw little. The room inside was gloomy, inhabited by pieces of dark, indistinct furniture. Crouching I gazed at the fading shine of black floorboards. It looked a weird, shrouded room — as cold and unwelcoming as the garden rustling behind me. Suddenly, on the boards, slightly to one side, something moved. Only an inch, no more. I was staring at a pair of feet encased in fat pink slippers! Each slipper, at its crest, trembling with a white fluffy tassel! Slowly I looked upwards, squinting through the glass. Staring back down at me from inside a cascade of pink — it was, I suppose, a night dress or fancy housecoat — staring down through twisting cigarette smoke, her face uncommonly pale, her eyes screwed tight, was Auntie Alex!

6

The shadow stood in the doorway, hesitated, and came towards me through the gloom. Turning my head on the pillow, I stared at the glisten of Aunt Wells' Lake of Galilee dress, heard its silken rustle as she drew up a chair. 'Gordon, why aren't you asleep?' but for once I knew that she was glad that I wasn't, that she wanted to stroke back my hair, press my hands, lean tenderly over the bed and talk. I knew her so well. Something new — elation perhaps, scarcely contained and still rising — breathed in the quiet room as strongly as her scent. Nor did she need to turn on the light. There was, for her purpose, light enough from the window. A large, faintly glimmering square, like silver water beside a quay. Surely a safe night harbour for both of us? For how I wanted to tell her, the instant she sat beside me! But how could I? Forbidden to leave the house, let alone trespass — Such horrors, Auntie Alex lurking amid dark furniture behind a window of Belle Lilac! What would Aunt Wells say if she knew? That dreadful public house woman — as she once had called her. That lady whose proudly exposed belly button Uncle had tickled with a gull's feather on Blackpool beach, though that Aunt didn't know! (Enough, perhaps, to know about the holiday. The infidelity. For Aunt Wells it must have been shattering. Her every sensibility outraged!) Not that I'd have known about the feather either if Auntie hadn't confided to me last summer, over ice cream in a café. And now, incomprehensibly, here she was again, pink garbed and bizarre at Belle Lilac. That window. Would I ever forget it? And though I'd immediately turned and run, and although there'd been no sound, no rattling of the glass or calling after me, and although, when I looked back from the gate, the house looked exactly as before — its windows dark, its curtains rumpled, desolate — I still felt shivery.

'A penny, Gordon, for your thoughts?'

'Uncle Conway,' I said, hurriedly, 'has gone to the Bear and Old Brunswick. I expect he's telling them about the Red Jesus in Spain.'

'Gordon! That was a most irreverent remark.'

And Aunt, shuddering, creaked on her chair, long thighs, under the blue dressed lake, swishing sharply.

Suddenly, as I lay, a tiny part of the duskiness round me seemed to change and harden, become an ominous frightening replica of the beauty spot on Auntie Alex's brow. A spot that, lurching, came suddenly towards me.

'Gordon, are you all right?'

'Yes, Aunt Wells,' I gulped. 'I thought I saw the dark move, that's all.'

'The dark, Gordon, does move. But too gradually for us to notice.'

Silence.

'Aunt Wells. Could — could Mr Price marry a lady with a dead husband?'

'My dear child! You mean could Mr Price marry a widow? Why, of course. If, that is, he's not married already, or is a widower. I imagine, though, that any man moving into that extremely large house must be married.'

What was it really like, I wondered? Being grown up, married? Able to look at, and tickle, ladies' belly buttons.

'Wouldn't you like to hear about the little country mission that I visited this evening? It might interest you.'

I hesitated. 'Oh, all right, Aunt Wells.'

'You're sure? I wouldn't want to waste my breath.'

'I'm sure, Aunt Wells.'

Aunt gave a deep, relieved sigh.

'The mission hall, Gordon, was just behind a little cottage. High up a winding lane, beside a copse. Only a small simple place, made of wood with a window or two of coloured glass. And about twelve pews — well, long brown benches really — on each side. And at the front a little harmonium, beside the lectern. Oh no pulpit, as in a church, merely the lectern on a table,' and Aunt, entranced, lilted descriptively on: the green baize cloth on the little table, the huge, lambent lettered old Bible, the gold plaque to the mission founder on the wall, the open door through which, lumbering in brushed uneasy suits from the fresh spring evening, came the farmers with their sons and daughters. And the first song from the Sankey hymnal, rousing, fervent, with its see-saw chorus. And Mr Mattey, preaching, reading the first lesson while, from outside, the peaceful intrusion of the country — a cow's low deepening Mr Mattey's Amen, bleatings from distant lambs, the frequent, respectfully gentle breeze through the door that wasn't shut till halfway through the service. And later, during the final hymn before the sermon, one of the men, treading quietly in all that lusty singing, lighting the two oil lamps. And the sermon itself, with its text of love. And the solemn creaking of the benches and the lamplight and the beating of Aunt's own uplifted heart.

'That, Gordon, was why I didn't go to church this morning. I thought that the contrast between church, with its formality, and the mission, with its freedom of procedure and spirit, would be to the mission's detriment. But how silly we are! How empty our little flutterings, our fears. I did so enjoy it all — more than I can say.'

And Aunt, perhaps talking to herself more than she was to me, was silent at last. I had shut my eyes and, instead of blackness, blue against my lids. Lake blue. Galilee blue. Soothing, wonderful. Blue to splash in. Swim in. Drown in —

'I think I can even be of some service to Mr Mattey and the other trustees of that little mission,' Aunt said abruptly. 'You remember Mr Edgar, do you not, Gordon?'

Out from drowsiness I jerked! Mr Edgar! As if I could ever forget the man who'd married Betty Hallet. Mild as milk, yet with horrid dark hair on his puny chest, a pale little man with deep dark eyes and a large, faintly sweating, pear shaped nose. Of course I remembered. Did he still tune pianos, I wondered? Did he still poke and fidget at the ageing yellow keyboards of our town? Did he still wear a hard dark hat and say, ad nauseam, 'Well done!' Did he still wear tall white collars and baggy jackets,

38

ride a bicycle and have slightly rounded shoulders? Did Betty — my eyelids rammed hurtfully shut — did Betty still love and kiss him?

'The nice little man who tuned our piano, married your friend Betty, and who was always so kind? Well, as it happens, the lady who plays the harmonium at the mission is leaving, and I said that I thought I knew someone who might be willing to take her place. I am sure that Mr Edgar would welcome the opportunity. It is not far off, he has his bicycle, and he was always saying that his work gave him little chance to play properly.'

'Silly old George!' I muttered. 'He couldn't play the spots off a bread pudding, Aunt Wells!'

And, for a moment, I wanted to hurt her, to say bluntly that I had just seen Auntie Alex! But I couldn't. Did I sense, somehow, that even in mentioning Betty — Auntie Alex's daughter — Aunt was being exceedingly brave? Although, true enough, she'd always liked Betty, briefly though she'd known her.

'Well, now,' Aunt said, suddenly laughing. 'We shall see. In fact, I thought that tomorrow, after tea, we might walk round together and see him. It's a good walk, but, given a fine evening, why not? If Mr Edgar *is* available, I would like Mr Mattey to know as soon as possible.'

Suddenly I dare not stir. It was as if the least movement or breath, even in the gloom, would betray me for ever! For, in seeing Mr Edgar, might I not also see Betty? Her brown pretty hair, the long beautiful arms — silky smooth as Aunt's dresses and nearly always adorned by a jolly bangle. Was she still as wonderful as I remembered? Would I still want to marry her — if, that is, I were grown up and she hadn't already married Mr Edgar? And, most important of all, did I really want to see her, with Aunt beside me, looking down at me, and Mr Edgar looking at me, and Betty herself looking at me? All of them, in some mysterious way, reading my mind? Perhaps I'd blush, go all pink and sticky hot. Did I want to hear her call me Gordon, feel her hands — dewy soft as the July daisies on our lawn before Sam's mowing — rumple through my hair? And what if she bent and kissed me?

Suddenly, in panic, 'I don't want to go, Aunt Wells,' I said, opening my eyes. 'I don't want to see Mr Edgar!'

But the chair by the bed was empty. No glimmer of blue, no hand or voice to touch me or respond. Only, across the darkness, a gently closing door.

7

Mr Edgar's house, which I'd not seen before, was the end dwelling of a small, elderly terraced row. The house itself looked quiet but friendly. The front door was partly open, and pretty, orange coloured curtains filled each window. A white Staffordshire china dog sat in the middle of the downstairs window, and some kind of small china ornament sat in the middle of the window above. This window — presumably a bedroom — came immediately under the roof. They really were low little houses. When Aunt Wells looked over the hedge Mr Edgar at once came to his feet, unfolding himself from a small mat on which he had been kneeling in a late afternoon patch of sunshine. He was wearing dark trousers gleamy-grained at the knees and, over a white shirt with the usual separate, high white collar, a matching waistcoat. If it hadn't been for the missing jacket — heaped like a fallen crow on the window ledge behind — upturned sleeves with dangling cuff links, and bicycle clips rusting away just above the ankles, the little man might have looked reasonably tidy, despite lank, rather greasy hair rubbing unkemptly at his collar rim.

'Well!' he gasped, dropping a trowel and hurriedly unpeeling his turned-back sleeves, 'this is splendid, splendid. An honour, to be sure. How are you? And you, too, young man,' he added quickly.

'Good afternoon, Mr Edgar,' Aunt said, extending her most gracious handshake, a regal white glide of bent gloved fingers. 'I see that you are planting bulbs. You set an example. Before we know it we shall all be planting. And weeding.'

'Ah yes, absolutely,' said Mr Edgar. 'All that dreadful spiky green. Backaching, to be sure. If only weeds could fly away like money!' He paused, misty-eyed. 'But it is a pleasure, a very real pleasure, to see both of you again!'

'Old sweaty pear nose,' I breathed, not quite loud enough for anybody to hear.

Then, with Aunt looking suspiciously at me, I tried to be at least mildly affable.

'Why are you working in bicycle clips?' I piped. 'Sam wears boots. So he can kick the plants on the head if they don't go in properly!'

'Gordon!' Aunt said, tiredly. 'Oh dear. I hardly feel that your gardening suggestions will commend themselves to Mr Edgar.'

'I fear not,' said Mr Edgar mournfully. 'Please, come in do.' And he opened the gate.

Obligingly, her hat bending as graciously as her fingers had done, Aunt stepped forward, but as she did so the gate slipped from Mr Edgar's earth-damp hand and shunted gently into her coat, the metal gate latch sharply pinging on one of her big new coat buttons!

'Oh dear,' said Mr Edgar, grabbing the gate in panic and trying again. 'The balance, all wrong! I think a hinge is weakening.'

Barmpot! I thought. You're the one with the weak hinge!

'Now, Mr Edgar,' Aunt said, briskly and warmly, but the little man stopped her by raising a mildly rebuking arm.

'George, please! After all this time—'

'I have always,' Aunt Wells said, perhaps more sternly than she intended, 'thought of you as Mr Edgar, just as I have always thought of your wife as Betty. It's curious how we become accustomed to particular thoroughfares, even of thought.'

'Exactly so,' said Mr Edgar, remorsefully. 'Creatures of habit. Indeed we are!'

'And ... how is Betty?'

'Oh, fine,' said Mr Edgar, blushing. 'In most excellent condition. But please, won't you come inside the house?'

And, taking his jacket from the ledge behind, he wriggled thankfully into it while Aunt aided by holding the top of one of the crow-black sleeves.

'First, if I may,' Aunt said, 'I would like to broach a little matter. Not of business exactly, more a matter of vocation. And be assured, dear Mr Edgar, that if the proposition doesn't interest you then I shall quite understand. But I thought of you, and felt that you should have the opportunity. First refusal, as it were.'

'Ah,' said Mr Edgar.

41

I chose that moment to draw the wrong conclusion.

'If Mr Edgar doesn't want them, Aunt Wells,' I gabbled, 'can I have them?'

They looked at me, Aunt with a look already bridled with reproach, Mr Edgar with that look of trepidation I remembered from last summer.

'If he refuses the plums you've brought him. Can I have them?'

'Oh.' Sighing, Aunt glanced down at her basket. 'I think our young man is being rather presumptuous, not to say greedy, Mr Edgar. You and Betty can make use of bottled plums, I trust?'

'Bottled plums!' said Mr Edgar, recoiling with uplifted hands, hairy nostrils shiny as ebony as they caught the light. 'Oh, well done!'

Well done! The same way of talking, the same barmy behaviour, and all over a few rotten yellow-green plums in a jar!

Disgruntled, leaving Aunt and Mr Edgar earnestly talking; what was it that they suddenly began to talk about? oh yes, the mission and that harmonium Aunt wanted Mr Edgar to play — away I turned, deciding that I should take the opportunity, while they were so fussily engrossed, to explore the rest of that small, unfamiliar garden.

On the fringe of the rank smelling grass that ran round the side of the house, I halted in surprise. Something half hidden, something brown, was propped between the grass and the corner of the house. Leaning forward I saw that it was a young, strangely motionless owl.

Glancing over my shoulder I saw that Aunt and Mr Edgar were still engrossed. Why call them anyway, I thought? They'd only become officious. Bending down I peered with interest at the drowsy bird. I'd not seen an owl so close before. The nearest had been in the dark, perched on the high telegraph-wires outside my window. Staring into my bedroom as if it could actually see me staring back. Just like one of our mantelpiece clocks, its night fierce eyes the clock face holes where the winding and chiming keys were put. And this smaller one in the grass no different. Squat, clock-like, needing only a ticking to ruffle it into measured life. Yes, I thought suddenly, feeling a queer little chill, I'd pick it up — if I could. Why I felt such courage I didn't really know.

Perhaps it was a legacy of the owl on the wires, the strange feeling of communication which — though probably felt only by me — had filled the slow mysterious minutes of the night. Yes, I'd pick it up, and — glowing idea! — take it to show to Betty. Why not? She'd understand. If it couldn't fly she would certainly know how to help it fly. And, armed with the owl as a diversion, what better way of meeting Betty again anyway?

The bird, as I picked it gingerly up, remained dormant. Only the hoods moved, briefly revealing brilliant eyes.

Another look round at the two on the tiny front lawn, talking away, and then, owl in both hands, I nudged through the open front door into a fusty tiny passage. An open door on my left showed a small room. Dark, varnished wallpaper, dark, tall dining chairs. An oval mirror — its glass dowdy from smoke from the grate below — hung listlessly. Against the far wall — its wanly cushioned stool almost touching the table behind it — was a piano. Only unlit coloured candles in brass brackets relieving the formal, unremitting rosiness of the old instrument. Also part of the room's cramped space, a dark blue, three-piece suite. On a thick dusty arm of one of these comfy but suffocating chairs lay a box of chocolates, but when, carefully balancing the owl, I peered inside, I saw that every chocolate but one had gone. Cautiously, still balancing the owl, I bent my head until my nose was rustling in the empty sweet papers. Moulding my lips around the surviving chocolate, I drew it up into my mouth with a noisy suck. Lovely coffee cream! A flavour slightly spoilt however, when, looking round, I saw a photograph of Auntie Alex on top of a wireless set just behind the door! A younger Auntie Alex — without a beauty spot — curly haired and spry. The owl and I jerked uneasily — the owl shuddering because I shuddered. Recovering my breath, I stepped critically over for a closer look. Even in this old picture, Auntie's indefatigable bosom was more than hinted at!

Returning promptly to the narrow little passage, I stood hesitating. Suddenly, from behind the door at the end, I heard the sound of splashing water and a voice, crooning Red Sails in the Sunset. Shivers ran all through me.

The door, as I edged it open with my left shoe, creaked brusquely. Still holding the little owl, I stepped inside.

Betty, with her back to me, and with only a sash of yellow flapping towel pitched around her middle, was leaning over, splashing impatiently with her hand at the steaming water in a long zinc bath. Owl forgotten, I gazed spellbound at her rear, where the towel was tied like a bow just above her buttocks — such pretty buttocks, the first belonging to a lady I ever saw, the lovely cleft between them a pale pearly valley that ran right round under the knotted towel and out of sight. As she came fully upright again the valley closed somewhat, making me wish my hand were clasped inside it, being warmly squeezed.

She must have heard the creaking of the door.

'I simply must have a tub, Georgie pet, else I shan't sparkle,' she said. 'So don't molest me, please. Especially with your hands all earthy.'

Then she turned and saw me. She gasped. The owl and I stood staring — well, at least I stood staring.

Baskets, loaves and fishes! I kept thinking stupidly. And the coffee taste, curiously resurrected, lying with new rich force across my curled-up tongue!

'Gosh, Gordon, you really startled me! What a conjuror's rabbit you are for coming out of nowhere! Just for a second I thought it was some strange little boy. And what on earth are you doing with an owl?' And Betty, completely unselfconscious despite her semi-nudity, took the somnolent bird gently from my hands and held it close, between her breasts. And there it hung as if presiding — that quaint, silent clock of a bird, its eyes still hooded, its breath quiescent, between two firm, small breasts, each moving evenly, palely, against its lofty plumage.

'Didn't — didn't you know it was me?' I gulped.

'Oh, Gordon, I'd almost forgotten you! It seems such a long long time since last summer.' Just for an instant, Betty looked up from the owl. 'Oh dear, you never did come to my wedding, did you?'

That was true. I'd heard only that there had been a wedding. Aunt Wells had been invited, but had declined to go.

'And suddenly here you are, with this little pet in your arms. Gosh, isn't it sweet?' And, utterly absorbed, Betty peered down at the strange small creature with the masked eyes. My own eyes, far from hooded, studied, wonderingly, the tips of her breasts, the spreading, minutely rippled crowns — almost the colour of my favourite bubble gum.

'Oh!' she said suddenly, as if coming to her senses. 'What am

44

I thinking of, standing here. Thank goodness it *was* you and not the rent man!'

The rent man! For a moment I was shocked.

'We don't pay rent,' I said. 'And I only have a bath once a week. We've got a bathroom. With a geyser over the bath. Aunt Wells says we're lucky to be so modern. She's outside now, talking on the lawn.'

'Of course. Your Aunt's with you!'

And something in Betty changed. Suddenly she wore a little fretful frown and didn't seem to be seeing me at all.

'I must dash. Sorry, pet. But because you've been so good about the owl, you can have a chocolate. There's one in a box in the room up the passage.'

Left alone — Betty, without surrendering her feathered charge, had grabbed some clothes and vanished behind a curtain in the corner, her bare feet padding quickly upstairs — I stood looking guiltily down at the bath. What had I done? Exactly what Aunt Wells always said I shouldn't do. I had forgotten to knock before entering a room, and that, especially if the room were in a strange house, would have been enough to turn Aunt's hair white. 'Gordon,' I could almost hear her saying. 'Once more you've transgressed. Will you never surmount your demon of carelessness?'

'But I was holding an owl, Aunt Wells,' I could hear myself replying. 'You can't knock with your feet! And it was only a kitchen, anyway.'

What a splendid answer. Of course! A kitchen wasn't a room. Not a proper room. Especially when it had a zinc bath in it! And, bending, I touched the water. It was cooling rapidly. Why, I wondered, did it seem so different from my bath water at home? Was it just the scent? Everything that ladies did seemed so much more fragrant. Of course the water wasn't used, but even if it had been, hard to imagine it as other than it was, frisky and clear as blown bubbles. Uncle Conway and I — we just turned water grey and nasty.

Footfalls, this time shod and ringing, and Betty, in a sleeveless red dress with a white belt, came brushing through the curtain. She had a cigarette in her mouth, and carried the owl.

'What I'm going to do with this young shaver I don't know,' she said, pausing, 'but something must be done. Poor little thing.' And off she went, out and along the passage into the garden.

From just inside the front door I watched her stop by Aunt and Mr Edgar. Both, on seeing the bird, exclaimed, Aunt opening her mouth with astonishment, breathing, 'Well, I never,' Mr Edgar blinking and waving his hands and saying, 'An owl, to be sure. Well, I never did!'

'I really must be off,' said Betty, after a few moments. 'We've a neighbour who knows about birds. I only hope he's in.'

And she was gone, just like that, in a blur of red dress and white belt — past the low hedge and out of view.

'Oh dear,' said Mr Edgar, looking slightly awry. 'You really must excuse her for rushing off. Most unfortunate. I really do apologise.'

'Now, Mr Edgar,' Aunt Wells said warmly, patting the little man's black fluttering sleeve. 'Your wife has a tender heart. Not many young women would be so concerned. I think you're to be congratulated — Betty's a fine girl. Quite unlike — '

'Just so, just so,' said Mr Edgar hastily. Proudly, as if Betty were still in view, he looked away up the street. 'But congratulations I do deserve, I really do. That heart of my wife's — touched by anything. Gracious, yes. Especially anything diminutive. Perhaps,' and Mr Edgar grew suddenly pink with speculation and discovery, the bloom on his pear-shaped, peculiar nose more than ever a gladsome dewy shine, 'perhaps that's why she married me!'

Irately, turning — what a sprig of mint he was, daft as well as small! — back I went along the passage to the kitchen. This time, ignoring the weakly steaming bath, I went straight to the corner, drew aside the curtain, and looked up the narrow stairs. Why not? I thought. Betty wouldn't be back for some time, and Aunt and Mr Edgar were fully occupied. Just a quick look round, a glance in the bedrooms. Up I went, three quaking stairs at a time. At the top, like a stuffy, darkly wallpapered box, a tiny landing. Opening a door, I looked warily inside. Betty's bedroom! Drooping from the pink, fluffy bedspread was the yellow towel. Beside it, obviously waiting to be tidied away, lay a stiff white gentleman's collar. Its vast, sloppily hanging stud green with perspiration. Ignoring this abomination I picked up the towel, then rather quickly put it down again. Crumbly rough, slightly scented, too intimate to hold! After a moment, still awestruck, I looked up. Just beyond the bed, on the white painted window ledge, was the ornament first glimpsed from the pavement

46

outside. A small, glittery, cheap-china mermaid, the end of her tail half lost, half swathed, in a swirl of bright curtain.

At first I didn't know why that concisely-fashioned, black and white little object should have such an effect. Then, after a moment, moving to the window, I did know why. She was like Betty! The slender arms were like Betty's arms — I saw again Betty's arm, winter-pale, dipping down to splash the water. The mermaid's dapper dazzling little shoulders were like Betty's shoulders, and even the small china breasts — really no more than slight protuberances with a dab of colour in their centres — brought to mind those other mounds, marvellously different from the painted china though they'd been. Thoughtfully, I ran a finger to and fro across the hard fleeting breasts of the mermaid. What else brought Betty back? Each tiny finger with its tip of red, the slight, daintily curving neck. Even the hair, short and brown — wasn't a mermaid supposed to have long straight hair, as if just out of the sea? If only, instead of giving her a fishy tail black as the hair in Mr Edgar's nostrils, they'd put a yellow towel around her!

How long I stood there, gazing, touching, marvelling — was coffee cream flavour suddenly back in my mouth as though it had never been away? — I could not judge. But suddenly, looking up, I saw Aunt Wells and Mr Edgar in the garden below. They had evidently seen me standing in the window, for they were gazing up with amazement, Mr Edgar nervously flexing his piano practised hands, mouth open as if about to sing, Aunt Wells frowning and gripping her basket with the jar of bottled plums. In a turmoil — had they seen me stroking the mermaid, what if they guessed my thoughts? — I turned confusedly, half fell over the bed, grabbed the first object to hand, righted myself, pushed my head through the window, and, waving the object belligerently in the fading brightness of the early springtime air, yelled:

'There's a horrid collar here. It's grimy on the inside with a horrid stinking stud. Why don't you buy Mr Edgar a nice new collar stud, Aunt Wells, instead of giving him plums?'

47

8

The following evening, at six o'clock exactly, the bell and knocker of our front door erupted in a curious irascible duet. Uncle was drinking off the effects of a quarrel in the study, shoes off, pudgy feet in short brown socks — suspender clips scowling on the white goosy flesh — up on the desk between his little clock and a sheaf of bare paper. He'd been there since five o'clock. 'Kiss me, friendly flask,' I'd heard him roaring, hoping no doubt that Aunt would hear. 'Kiss my mouth with fire, ferment my belly, stoke my vitals! Fill my bladder with spirituous delight!' Then a bit later, a burst of no less inspired singing, a lyric of his own matchless making. 'Yo ho ho and a bottle of gum. Gum, rum, gum, rum, gum a-rum rum! Oh it's my delight, on a rum-filled night, to gum the parks with rain ... '

'The daft black-bruised banana!' Sam said loudly, hobbling past the french windows of the dining room where he knew Aunt, fraught, was arranging and rearranging her collection of cut glass. 'They'll be a-hearing of him in town square. Wants clapping in a barrow and a-carting off!'

Sam was chiefly to blame for the whole unhappy atmosphere. Turning up after tea he had told Aunt with huge, hand-rubbing, nostril-whistling glee, that the rumour about that Mr Price and Belle Lilac was rubbish. 'Dunno where he got it from,' he said, adding contradictorily, 'It's them at the Bear and Old Brunswick having him on. Always in his cups there, ain't he? Just what they'd do, them at the Bear. A-knowing his politics.'

'Sam, please!' Aunt said angrily, which meant that she thought he was probably right.

'It's a Mrs Ballet or Mallet — I never caught it proper. A winnow.'

'Widow, Sam, widow. To winnow means taking chaff out of grain.'

'Sounds right to me,' said Sam, sharply flushing. 'Women what have laid their good seed to rest — their a-grain six feet under — and are the chaff what's left up top.'

Flustered, Aunt had gone into the house and found Uncle Conway goodhumouredly stroking the bare arms and tickling the upraised armpit of the urn-carrying Grecian lady in the hall.

'Really, Conway! Your most valuable piece. One day you'll break it.'

'Damn it, woman, you're always making out I'm clumsy. Look at my hands. Steady as rocks!'

And Uncle, aggrieved, held out his hands.

Ignoring Uncle's fingers — trembling slightly from the first libations of the day — Aunt said briskly, 'Apparently that rumour about Belle Lilac and Mr Price was all nonsense. A widow is living there.'

Uncle turned puce.

'A widow? Who the devil says so?'

'Sam says so.'

Whether genuinely, or theatrically, Uncle Conway belched.

'I think, Conway, that Sam's reliability is less in question than that of your acquaintances at the ... '

'The Bear and Old Brunswick?' Uncle goaded.

'Be that as it may,' Aunt said, trying to keep calm, 'it's made me feel ashamed. What sort of neighbours are we? What must she think? Several days now since she moved in, and still we haven't called. I must say I'm amazed, though. A widow at Belle Lilac! All alone in that extremely large house.'

'Well, I'm not calling, Wells. And, if you've any damn sense, you won't either.'

'Yes, Gordon, what is it?' said Aunt, wearily.

'Nothing, Aunt Wells,' I muttered.

'Oh, Conway, please reconsider. It would be so pleasant if we could all call. As a family. Yes, Gordon, you too.'

I held my breath.

But Uncle was already making for the stairs. 'Sorry, Wells, but no! I make my stand on principle. Damn it, you of all people should understand that. It's so blasted menial! Turning up cap in hand on someone's doorstep. Look at us, we're your new neighbours, aren't we nice? Aren't we lovely respectable people? Bah! There's more going on in the world than that kind of sickening slop.'

49

'Such as that wretched unnecessary war in Spain, I suppose?' Aunt shouted.

'Unnecessary?' Uncle ranted, turning on the landing to wave a furious fist. 'Unnecessary! The war in Spain! For God's sake, woman. Look up from your Bible! Forget about Moses. Forget the snivelling Ten Commandments. Forget about the Jewish race begetting itself! Forget about Judas Iscariot. Face to the sun, Wells! Be a warrior's wife. Embroider me a tunic to die in! We're fighting to make Spain part of the new European order. We're fighting to kick out the Red plague. We're fighting to capture Madrid. If Madrid falls, the Republic falls! Listen, can't you hear the bombs? Can't you smell the smoke in the streets? Is your Wellsian nose beyond the odour of our conflict? Our troops attack. The damn Madrilenos in their trenches hold us at bay. No pas-ar-an! They shall not pass! No pas-ar-an! They shall not pass! And behind them that Red witch, La Pasionaria or whatever they call her. The Communist. Spurring them on, more than any government, any general! But we'll beat her. Our sweat won't be in vain. Our — our arms, our hopes, are high. Our —' Pause. 'Damn it, we're fighting, woman. That's all I know. Fighting!'

Beside me Aunt was briefly silent, as if something of Uncle's fervour had affected even her. Then, recovering, 'I shall require your underwear tonight, Conway. For the dirty-washing bag. While you glorify war, I have a house to run.'

And Aunt, in quiet umbrage, fled to her cut glass, while Uncle, after slamming his study door, sang the little song about rain and rum gumming up the park.

The summons! The duet of bell and knocker shrilling, thudding, through the hall.

It was strange how the three of us, as though sensing trouble, crept each from our retreats to the outskirts of the hall, Uncle dimly observable at the head of the first landing, Aunt hovering in the dining room doorway, while I, blinking and uneasy, peered at the front door from behind a tall, statuesque curtain.

Again the summons, only this time not in duet but isolated bursts, first the knocker, then the bell.

'Really,' I heard Aunt Wells murmur as, coming to life, she moved at last from the shelter of the dining room doorway. 'We're not deaf!'

Nor were we blind, Aunt Wells and I. Uncle, still on the landing, may not have immediately seen — but Aunt and I at once recognised the opulently dressed, hatless, cigarette smoking lady in the porch, as Auntie Alex!

Auntie Alex, bright as her roguishly painted mouth, made no bones about the reason for her visit.

'Blimey, dear, you look surprised. Haven't you heard? Hasn't the little lad told you?'

Aunt Wells, shocked as she must have been at being called dear by Auntie Alex for the first time in their sketchy, painful acquaintanceship, was for once not quite in command, either of herself or the doorstep. Out went her hand automatically, a white, slender betrayal of her brain, and Auntie, with a jolly, elbowing motion of her half bare arm, grabbed it and shook it in the air as if it were a cocoanut being checked for milk. 'Wells, isn't that your name? That's what Conway always called you anyway. I'll bet you think I'm cheeky, don't you? A cheeky monkey. Acting as if we were bosoms. Bosom pals, that is. But I hope we will be, dear. You see, I'm the new one.'

'New one?' Aunt Wells whispered. She had turned ashen, one worried arm raised to her brow, the other swaying for support.

'The new one. The belle in Lilac! Least that's how my late dear hub, Noel deceased, would have put it. Alex, he'd have said, poet that he was, you're the belle in Lilac, the lovely lady of the manor. Not that Belle Lilac's a manor exactly but, as I said to Betty, manors aren't everywhere, not even hereabouts they're not. Not that Noel was Willy Wordsworth neither. Never got his immortals printed on paper, like that one did. Just a natural poet, blowing out his words with fag smoke over the washing up, or over the daily paper — which was The Times, let me tell you. None of your beastly yellow press muck for my Noel. Too aspiring to the heights, too much a genius to sink that low.'

Somehow, without having been invited in, Auntie Alex was in the hall, swinging her handbag, looking for somewhere to stub her cigarette, and shaking loose a stone from one of her bright green court shoes — all at the same time. Her thickly powdered cheeks, with rouge glowing volcanically beneath the powder, looked new as Turkish delights fresh from the box; she had not discarded either her beauty spot, under curly resilient hair, or her plump, beginning-to-swell throat. The dress lower down looked unsuitable for spring, too summery and youthful, with a wide low

51

neckline and layers of frail pink and white pleats. When she pulled up from adjusting her shoe her breasts seemed to protrude and rock alarmingly.

'Wouldn't say no to a sit down and a cup of tea. Or a glass of something,' she said, staring at all the doors as if she were wondering which one to plunge through. 'These lovely green shoes are throttling me!'

Without a word Aunt Wells bent, recovering the stone from the lushly patterned carpet. She came upright just in time to see another outrage, Auntie's cigarette hovering over, and then disappearing into, a small, apparently empty wall vase. There was the dreadful hiss of water scorched from its slumbers.

'Whoosh!' said Auntie Alex cheerfully. 'Talk about fire water! Which I wouldn't say no to. Gosh, have I been working myself dry! The truth is I'm still all at sixes and sevens. Still getting tidy, even if there isn't too much furniture as yet. Betty thinks I'm mad, moving into such a big house that I can't even furnish it. Well, I'll collect, I told her. A chair here, a table there, a nice antique commode for the bedroom for when I'm ill. The young know nothing, do they, Wells? Oh lordy, no. No patience for collecting. Wanting the world all in a minute, like toads sucking up pond water. Thank God I'm middle-aged.'

The stairs creaked. Uncle Conway's socks descended once, twice. I saw his face. It was a strange, pulsating purple-grey, while his one protuberant eye appeared to be experiencing great difficulty in aligning itself with the other protuberant eye.

'It — it's Mrs Hallet, Conway,' Aunt Wells said unnecessarily, in a voice so weak and remote it seemed to float down from the ceiling. 'She — she has moved into Belle Lilac!'

'Oh I'll speak plain,' said Auntie Alex, casually rubbing, with the ball of her pallid thumb, the Grecian lady's proud straight nose. 'It's what I've always wanted, this neighbourhood. Not that I haven't always been part of it, with the Arms and that. But run a licensed house and people think you're common. Enough's enough. I said it at Christmas, when I was ill as a shroud, and I say it now. So I left. Was away before the little Christmas tree had left the bar. Oh it wasn't easy, leaving the Arms, forsaking the trade, the company, but I always had the money to be a lady, so why not? Why not, I said to Betty, why stand behind a bar and be despised when I've got the money to make my own life, buy a good private house and be somebody. Not to mention the saving of my health, health being more precious than rubies. After all, it's what dear Hallet would have wanted, bless his poor deceased heart. Yes, dear, I will sit down. Talk's better sitting down.'

If we were suddenly in one of the rooms, amongst chairs and cushions as plump and genial as Auntie Alex herself it was, I suppose, because Aunt Wells, fearing for the safety of the china with that pale heavy thumb jabbing everywhere, again took action, albeit automatic poker-faced action. As for me, I was amazed. Never had I seen Auntie Alex in such good humour. Gone the old sour strain. She fairly flounced and purred, looking at Aunt from under her thick black lashes with almost sisterly regard. Uncle Conway she ignored. While Aunt Wells sat reluctantly down he stood fidgeting pathetically on shoeless feet in the doorway, looking ready to topple.

'And my little man!' she said, looking suddenly at me. 'How are you, son? Come and be kissed!'

I glanced at Aunt Wells but she only nodded, her eyes somehow lost, departed. Dazedly, for nothing now seemed quite real for me either, I edged across the room. At once Auntie seized me. I felt her knees digging into my stomach, her plump moist hands gripping my ears. Over I fell, my face brushing her bosom, smelling — and seeing — its twin halves, big and ivory coloured and astoundingly soft, but the kiss, landing on the side of my neck, on my rear hairline below the one ear, wasn't so pleasant, reeking of something very much like the something that I knew Uncle Conway kept in his flask.

'Fish baskets!' I muttered, writhing and turning away. 'Don't like stinks!'

But Auntie Alex, laughing, gripped me at the rear under my jacket, using my braces to yank me back against her. Suddenly I was a prisoner, her knees great gentle cannons keeping me in place.

'So, after leaving the Arms at Christmas, and while I looked around for somewhere to live, I stayed with Betty,' gabbled the loquacious, newly benign Auntie Alex, her warm fruity breath stirring the hairs on my cropped little neck. 'Not that staying with Betty worked, I'll say that. Only two bedrooms, one on top of the other, so to indelicately speak. A mere splinter of a landing in between! And with Betty newly wed, let's say I began to worry about the wall plaster.'

Aunt Wells closed her eyes. Tightly.

'That George Edgar, artistic hands. Handy hands. Well, a piano tuner! Nothing much to look at, that I'll grant — not like my late dear handsome — but when you watch him turn on a tap, or cut the roast beef, or put a Sunday hanky in his breast pocket — '

And Auntie Alex, apparently lost for words if not for breath, fairly steamed against my neck.

'Where was I? Oh yes. Artistic, handy hands. The Almighty's greatest blessing, especially to a married man.' And, though I couldn't see her fully I knew her head had shifted sideways, that she was looking towards Uncle Conway as he filled the doorway like some hapless dolorous marionette. 'Or, for that matter, to any man as aspires to love a woman ...'

No one else spoke. The warm breath, undeterred, blew deeply in my hair.

'So round I looked. For a house. And when I saw Belle Lilac, oh I knew! Not that Betty did. Half a mo, mother, she said, it's too big for one. Don't be a silly monkey, I said. I shall have my daily woman in to clean, singing on her knees, scrubbing with her arms and elbows like dailies do. I shall have my visitors, the best of the clientele from the old days at the Arms, the *gentlemen*, and above all, I said to Betty, I shall have my new neighbours, new good class friends I can visit and respect.'

'What did Betty say to that?' asked Aunt Wells faintly. She must have been remembering yesterday, Betty's abrupt departure with the owl, and her non-return even though she, Aunt Wells, had lingered talking to Mr Edgar for another good half hour. Undoubtedly, knowing of her mother's past relationship with Conway, the girl was embarrassed. Even ashamed perhaps. For whether Aunt Wells knew of that relationship or not, her mother's action, in planking herself at Belle Lilac, must have seemed, to Betty, the apex of insensitivity. There, in fact, lay the only slightly mitigating factor. For certainly Auntie Alex — like Betty — couldn't have been sure that Aunt Wells even knew of the affair — it had ended before Aunt found out. Of the subsequent quarrel between husband and wife, of Aunt's forgiveness of Uncle, she almost certainly knew nothing. Not that such subtleties really affected the situation as far as Aunt Wells was concerned. Here, before her, sat Conway's former mistress — that much *she* knew — and every fibre of her spare, lightly freckled skin must have itched with the impact, dire and shattering, of meeting at last her new neighbour —

'What did Betty say?' Auntie Alex repeated. 'Lordy, Wells, we've only spoken once before, you and I — in disgusting insalubrious circs outside the Arms when your hub was being sick — and you were as snooty as I was vexed — men in their cups! no advert for a pub I'll tell you — and it does me good to hear you speak so naturally of Betty as to call her by her Christian. Well, what *did* Betty say? Dutiful daughter that she is, flesh of me and flesh of Noel, she had to admit it was up to me, that if I wanted a big house then a big house I should have. So I bought Belle Lilac. Not that it was in quite the condition I would of expected. The previous people — those wrinkled as prunes old virgins, that Miss Young and Miss Cuthbert — not quite the ladies I would have thought!'

'What do you mean?' Aunt Wells said sharply.

Behind me, as if vacuuming my neck, Auntie sniffed long and abrasively. 'For one thing, whisper it, they left things.'

'Left things, Mrs Hallet?'

'In corners, dear. They left things in corners.'

In the doorway Uncle Conway shifted uneasily from one short leg to another. Slowly Aunt Wells raised her handkerchief, touching it to the delicate cream of her nostrils almost with fear, or at any rate foreboding. Somewhere out of sight behind a half drawn curtain a blown leaf tapped restively on the window. Even the corners of the cushions seemed suddenly to twitch.

'What *things*? If one may ask?'

'Bunny balls, dear. Rabbit droppings!' Auntie paused to take a dramatic, confidential breath. 'Not what you'd expect to find at all.'

'I don't believe it!' said Aunt Wells hotly. 'I really do not. Oh I know they kept rabbits — for the wool of course — but I never saw any rabbits in the house. Not at any time.'

I felt Auntie Alex's knees suddenly harden in the middle of my rear.

'I know a hundred year old rabbit dropping when I see one, dear,' she said, grimly.

'Rubbish!' Aunt Wells rapped while Uncle, for once a complete non-participant, more than ever an unhappy, mottled little man, shuddered in the doorway. 'The Misses Young and Cuthbert were ladies, real ladies. They kept Belle Lilac in scrupulously good order. I was proud to be their friend.'

'Well they ain't ladies in my opinion! What kind of ladies bring in bunnies for a cuddle, and let 'em mess all over the skirting board at the same time? I tell you I know all about messes, I've seen enough in my time with the vomiting brigade, those who can't hold their cups. Mentioning no names,' with another shift of the head, another glance at Uncle Conway.

'I will not,' said Aunt Wells, 'listen to insults directed at dear friends of mine, one now passed away. I am afraid, Mrs Hallet, that you have gone too far!'

'Gone too far? Gone too far?' said Auntie Alex, suddenly jigging me backwards and forwards as if I were a battle shield. 'How dare you? Here I come, looking for a welcome, and do I get it? What a neighbourhood! Only welcome I've had so far is from the little man here. Put me a magazine through my door he did. Heard somebody yelling. Scared me at first — thought it was the local vicar after my virtue — but then I saw *him* in the garden. Little fellow! Sweet little devil!' And, screwing me round, Auntie Alex — though doubtless only in order to infuriate Aunt Wells — kissed me again, clenching me against her bosom. This time I thought I felt her tongue, its tip snaking briefly out to touch my own wildly flailing tongue. And when, shaken, I let her thrust me back, just for a second, the most intangible, the most fleeting of seconds, a strange thing happened. I saw beyond that thickening face to an Auntie even younger than the one in the photograph in Betty's house. I saw the way she must have been when Noel first kissed her. Soft and kittenish, tender as her tongue —

'I'll go then,' said Auntie Alex, struggling up. Her face, and voice, were suddenly vicious, the pupils of her eyes tiny venomous black cherries. 'It's not been what I expected, but then, you're not a lucky woman, are you, Wells? Never known,' her breath, hot now, blew down and across me as strongly as if I were outside a public house, inhaling the stuffy air over opened cellar flaps, 'the right kind of hands, have you? Not the sort of hands every woman should know. Lovers' hands. Hands with six fingers and no thumbs, so to speak. Hands that make a woman's tit tops stand on end and sing!'

After Auntie Alex had gone, making her own way to the front door — Uncle Conway leaping panic-stricken to one side as, slightly wobbling, she plunged in his direction — the house was oddly different. Aunt Wells, without moving, sat on in her chair, silent, erect, her gaze lost somewhere in the countless cushions and lengthening shadows — as beleaguered, as trapped in her own home — her way of life as threatened — as the Spanish Republican government, and its forces, in bombed besieged Madrid.

'Oh, Conway,' she whispered at last, 'How could you have ever — With that woman ... '

And Uncle, stumbling across the carpet, nearly falling over a tumbled cushion, sinking helplessly into the nearest chair.

'I don't know, my darling. I can't think why. It — it shouldn't have ever happened. God knows why it did.'

9

The following morning, brisk and cheeky as the spring breeze nagging and twitching at the hem of her dress, Auntie Alex was back in our porch.

'Yes, it's me, Wells,' she cried, stepping quickly into the hall. 'How could I not come, that sorry I am for yesterday. A trifle in my cups, that was my trouble. A trifle in my cups, and like a disgraceful ventriloquist's doll saying things I didn't really mean, that weren't in my brain at all. It was the devil prompting, no doubt of that. And you a lady! What you must have thought! Oh lordy, the sleep I haven't had, twisting and turning until my toes turned grey, and wondering how I could say sorry. Here, dear,' opening the handbag over her arm and drawing something out, 'take this. Only a tiny peace offering, but if you'll take it ... '

Aunt Wells, who from her appearance hadn't slept either, looked shattered, with a quite untypical quiver to cheek and mouth. Yet though quickly gone, fleeting as a ripple on water, it seemed to leave a legacy across her face, a pale lake of suppressed feeling, of anger contained only by some desperate spiritual instinct.

'Like I say, only a small thing, but if you'd like it ... '

It was no larger than a biscuit, a tiny maroon volume bound in softest suede. It had a well thumbed, faded look.

'Love poems by Ella Wheeler Wilcox,' Auntie said. 'All the rage once, wasn't she? With her poems of passion — My Noel gave me that, sloppy loving devil, in our salad days. Was a time, I'll admit, when I wouldn't have parted with that, not for all the tea in China, but lately, well lately things have changed. It's as though,' she added mysteriously, looking into the darker corners of the hall as if expecting to see someone, 'it's as if he isn't dead at all. That's how it's been lately, as if he wasn't dead at all, and all the sentimental old keepsakes don't mean the same. How can they? Not with him still abroad, so to speak. Oh lordy, Noel my man, my late loving flesh, are you still there, thinking poems about me, longing for my scent, my arms? What a thought, eh Wells, what a thought!'

I don't think Aunt Wells was really thinking at all. Like the Grecian lady, frozen with urn on head, she stood holding the little book of verse, quite as frozen, quite as dead.

'Not at school, little man?' Auntie said, looking at me.

'You'll never be the Canterbury archbishop, bless his holy name. You'll be a dustbin man when you grow up, that's what you'll be.'

'I've been sick,' I announced, proudly. 'All green and brown, with spots of yellow!'

'Ah, bile the vile, as my dearest used poetically to say. Which reminds me,' Auntie Alex said, producing a cigarette from that stiff shiny capacious handbag. 'I need a commode. Betty's always saying I should have a commode. In case of illness. So I was wondering, Wells, if you had a commode I could buy second-hand. Well, you know what you're getting with a second-hand one. Tested, true and tried, so to speak.'

I knew all about commodes because Aunt Wells had two, in rooms upstairs. One made of cane, with a cushion red as a raspberry over the seat, the other made of teak, dark and strong as the tall-winged angels carved all across the arms and back.

'But you've got a chamber pot!' I said accusingly, remembering my one and only visit to Auntie's musty, purple-draped bedroom at the public house. 'Under your bed. At the York Arms.'

'Had a chamber pot at the Arms, little man. It's at Belle Lilac now. Not the same though, are they? Hate chamber pots, really. Not genteel.'

'Yours was full, anyway!' I said.

'Gordon! I simply cannot believe my ears,' Aunt said, coming suddenly alive, holding a hand to her head while in her other hand the little book dipped and trembled. 'You will apologise at once to Mrs Hallet. And prepare to accept punishment later.'

'So that's that,' said Auntie, breezily. 'All forgiven and forgotten. Eh, Wells? You and me, I mean. Yesterday. All forgiven?'

A conference hall for statesmen, redolent with polished tables and sombre pens and gleaming inkwells, as well as the solemn bald heads of the statesmen themselves, could not have assumed any greater importance than did our hall in that moment, with decision trembling on the brink. Yet for Aunt Wells there was really no decision to make. To react ungraciously to an apology, even if every word and gesture of that apology were as a breath of gall that caught at nose, throat, and even heart, how could she? The text on Mr Mattey's gun shop wall, the whispering gilt edges of her Bible, the dark pews of her church, the oil lamps of the little mission, even her best Sunday clothes waiting upstairs in the wardrobe to escape and join again in rustling, kneeling worship, were they not suddenly with her in the hall, the precious things, the reminding things that spoke of trial that must be borne, of faith somehow sustained, of courage, sublime and steady, in the face of outrage? And so Aunt looked down at the little book, with its sentimental, almost taunting poems of passion romantic and incomparable, of love to the strains of the Blue Danube Waltz and love to the strains of a waltz-quadrille, ballroom battlefields of long ago hearts, and she even smiled a little, a forlorn tiny smile.

'It's midmorning,' she said, suddenly, as if finally accepting what had to be. 'Please, Mrs Hallet, will you join me? A coffee and a biscuit would benefit both of us. And I — I do appreciate the book.'

Auntie Alex seemed to wriggle within her dress, to squirm with pleasure inside its bright blue vastness and big, saucy dots of white. 'That's kind of you, Wells. Honest. Takes a lady, I always say. I can see that you and I are going to be real pals. Chums of the bosom, as my late Noel once put it, his bare chest next to mine in bed. Which was in order, our being married with Betty already on the way.'

No one seemed to think, as we all three entered the large kitchen, of Uncle Conway. Had he gone out, or was he in his study? I don't think even Aunt knew and perhaps it didn't matter; if Uncle knew that Auntie Alex was present he would certainly not appear, nor could Aunt Wells have wished him to.

'May I introduce Mrs Hampton, who helps me with the housework? And Sam, who helps with the garden,' for Sam had just arrived, squeaking meanly in his tallest grubbiest boots. While the two helps stood together — Mrs H frowningly judicial as she gazed at Auntie's dress, Sam staring at the gaping neckline — Aunt Wells, determinedly calm — texts and pews and prayers still, no doubt, juggling dementedly in her assaulted yet resilient mind — took a sip of the coffee Mrs Hampton had already prepared.

'Excellent, Mrs Hampton. Beautifully hot. Did you want something, Sam?'

Sam glowered. 'Spring a-pruning on the roses, that's what I wants to do.'

'Whatever you think best, Sam.'

'And when you've finished, call on me,' said Auntie Alex blithely. 'I've some old vegetable beds could do with turning over. Belle Lilac, you know. The big house round the corner.'

'I know Belle Liluck,' Sam muttered. 'Known it all me days. But I ain't a-working there. Grief no.'

'Why not?' said Auntie Alex indignantly. 'Think I wouldn't pay you, is that it?'

Sam looked at her with interest. A long, dark, calculating look.

'Mice!' he said, suddenly nudging Mrs Hampton's ribs. Mrs H immediately seemed to lift herself compactly off the kitchen floor. A petrified cleaning lady rising to heaven on Ascension Day! When she came down she was gasping, cheeks puffed and pink, the blue ribbon across her bleached disordered hair shining through like stale confetti.

'Really, Sam!' Aunt Wells reproved.

'Mice at Belle Liluck, I mean,' growled Sam contemptuously. 'Whiffs like the underarms of sweatshop women, mice does. And that's Belle Liluck. A-smelling like women's hair nests!'

That Sam had never been in Belle Lilac in his life was something that even I knew — Miss Cuthbert and Miss Young had always regarded him with horror — but that was something Auntie Alex certainly did not know. Strangely, or not so strangely perhaps, Aunt Wells for once sat silent. Not even a quick, firm lift of eyebrow at such unabashed untruthful vulgarity! And who could blame her? She wasn't perfect. (She was giving Mrs Hallet coffee, but only in the kitchen. She was not contradicting Sam, even if the mention of mice defamed the Misses Young and Cuthbert as much as the alleged existence of rabbit droppings. Wasn't accepting the apology, and the little book of love poems, enough in one morning for any woman?)

'That man's a lying brute,' said Auntie Alex as Sam, followed by Mrs Hampton, stumped out. 'I haven't seen mice.' She shuddered. 'Hate the tiny perishers. If there's mice I'd have the army in, like a shot!'

'Will you have a biscuit, Mrs Hallet?' Aunt Wells asked, smiling thinly.

'Well, now,' said Auntie Alex, recovering somewhat and reaching for her coffee. 'what was I saying? Oh yes. About my late Noel being still abroad, wasn't that what I was saying?'

'Still abroad?' said Aunt Wells, frowning. 'I am afraid, Mrs Hallet, that I don't understand.'

'Well, not really abroad, since he's dead. Or is he dead? Because it really is uncanny, as I said to Betty.'

And Auntie Alex, eyes moist from smoke as the cigarette grew shorter in her mouth, rubbed a plump hand worriedly up and down her other forearm.

'It was such a shock. I opened this magazine, the one left me by the lad here, and there he was, his full page photo! My God, I thought, that's Noel! But it wasn't, it was this Spanish wallah. General Franco! But like Noel! My God yes, high in the forehead, that calm noble look like he was a creature apart; handsome, good strong eyebrows, good nose, moustache. It was uncanny, I tell you. Nearly had a heart attack I did. Only of course this Franco fellow was in uniform, which my dear one never was.'

Aunt Wells, looking as if she needed it, took a long gulp of coffee and closed her eyes.

'Uniforms,' she murmured, 'do not impress me, Mrs Hallet. Especially when worn by foreigners.'

'Had a sash round his middle, ever so nice. And you know what? It said that when Madrid was captured, he — Franco — wanted to enter on a white horse. Enter Madrid on a white horse! I ask you, only a gentleman could ever do that, could ride a white horse in triumph! Only Madrid hasn't fallen yet, so he hasn't done it,' Auntie ended, wistfully.

'Why horses,' said Aunt Wells bleakly, 'should be subjected to the purgatory of war I can't think. But it's been like that, all through history. One thinks of Richard III, that grossly maligned monarch, falling at Bosworth Field. His horse was white. As king's horses usually were.'

'There's a horse near us. In that field by the corner,' I butted in, looking challengingly at Auntie Alex. 'Dolly. She's white. Could your late dead husband ride *her*, do you think?'

'Not Noel, son, though, as I said, I'm tempted to think he lives again, but this general. Oh it's sent me Spanish barmy, it has. It's made me almost wish I'd never bought Belle Lilac. Should have bought a house with shutters, and a nice little balcony. Like they have in Spain. We had a gentleman patron at the Arms who'd been there before the Civil War. Lovely, he said, if you ignore all the bells for ever clamouring, and the skinny dogs running everywhere, and the caged birds — ugh, I'd hate that — and all the bleeding hearts, and Christs as common as advertisements for Bovril, begging pardon. And the funny way they carry on, he said. No carpets even in the best houses, just lovely parquet or marble flooring, and maids with rags on their feet — what a way to shine a floor, eh, Wells? — and courtyards with wrought iron gates and sometimes a fountain. Well, one consolation, Belle Lilac hasn't many carpets yet, so I'm half Spanish already!'

'I think that's where people are brown,' I said. 'In Spain. And you're not!'

Auntie laughed, affably, waving at me a friendly lance of grey smoke from the pink rump of her cigarette, and bestowing upon me a wink so pale and heavy that — except for the lashes sweeping salaciously at her rouged, powdered cheeks — it seemed exactly like a descending suet pudding.

'And who should know better that his Auntie's a lovely white all over, eh, son? However, as I was saying, I'm Spanish barmy. If only Belle Lilac had a courtyard that I could fill with geraniums in pots! I'd be that proud, that Spanish. The general himself could visit me. 'Noel,' I'd say, 'are you back? Is it you turned Spanish?' And if he wanted to open my shutters — Franco, that is — and make himself at home —' She sighed. 'Well, only fancy, isn't it, Wells, but nice, nice to dream.'

Aunt Wells, speechless, eyes still closed, was looking blindly down at her clasped hands. She seemed hardly to be breathing, she might herself have been a Spanish lady, fraught, riveted by prayer while, nearby, the wanton rolling guns of violation thundered on and on.

'Long live Franco, that's what I say. The sooner he wins the better!' Auntie Alex, too, suddenly closed her eyes. 'Oh God, on a white horse! Makes your tit — makes your pins and needles rise to even think of it!'

By now I was bored. Dare I ask Aunt Wells if I could be excused? Would she even notice if I left? Putting my hands behind my back I began edging, very slowly, towards the door. There I stopped, taking a last look at that abnormal kitchen scene, Aunt Wells still in an attitude of desperate prayer, looking unseeingly at her hands, Auntie Alex lost in fantasy and the smoke of a new cigarette, only her coal black beauty spot hard and real above her misty eyes. After a moment, taking courage, I pinched open the door and sidled through. The passage outside was empty, its dark walls somnolent. Perhaps only the air betrayed. It was a trifle acrid, smelling faintly of cigar smoke. Or was I, too, like Auntie Alex, merely dreaming?

10

Suddenly, rather like Auntie Alex in Belle Lilac, spring was full blown and established, full of arrogance and proud new colour. Whether Aunt Wells even noticed the shifts and fresh subtle growths of the young developing season was doubtful. Perhaps she only noticed, or at any rate only thought about, Auntie Alex. For there the woman was, perpetually on Aunt's doorstep — seemingly no excuse for calling overlooked. She was now the pestilential butterfly, her old skin (The York Arms) discarded, a plump shiny butterfly skimming — at times uncertainly, as if inebriated by fresh air and changed circumstances — our landscape, fluttering unwelcome tipsy wings in Aunt's face, stressing unbearably her new high-flying status as a lady of leisure. Unquestionably she had emerged into our lives in a way impossible before. And Aunt could do nothing. Except suffer. Rare now for her to pass Belle Lilac, she went the other way, and that way only after scrutinising the horizon for the enemy. True she carried off each unfortunate encounter with high courage, but each little ordeal of being conventionally bright and pleasant — even helpful — left its legacy. Yet to have moved was out of the question, an unthinkable capitulation. Why should she? She may have been fonder of the old house than she ever admitted, its rooms had yielded to her quick rustle and brisk hands a thousand thousand times, her shadow on the carpets, like a dark gentle brush down the years, was expected to continue; it was implicit in the way the house lived and breathed. Each threshold, dark or sunny, was now as much a part of her as Uncle Conway's early morning cough, or the old house martin's nest over the porch, or the dim elongated shine of her slender body in the taps of the old narrow bathroom. Better, surely, to learn to love Auntie Alex. But how? Doubtless each morning she planted seeds of prayer, hoping they would grow to perfection, but by nightfall the thorns of deep abhorrence were choking everywhere. Even Uncle Conway, still uncharacteristically subdued, eternally scuttling into shadows, felt the pinch. For if Aunt Wells couldn't feel warmth toward Alex she was equally hard put to find warmth for the husband who had brought her such travail.

Two escapes had Aunt that spring. One to nostalgia, for so long relegated to insignificance in her life, but now, perhaps, suddenly necessary — even if it meant reliving Great War memories, with that harrowing loss of a soldier sweetheart. Strange though, that part of that yearning for things past, an occasional dipping into the little suede book of love poems — her cuffs rolling and turning in a slow trim dance across her lap as she turned the pages — should have been instigated by Auntie Alex. Or were the poems (like the church up the avenue, or the local railway station, or the cobbles in town square) already poignantly familiar to Aunt from her own past, and their reappearance, no matter from what source, to be wistfully welcomed? Desolate Aunt. For it wasn't so much that Uncle had been unfaithful and that she must now bear the proximity of his sin (bad enough having to just look at Auntie Alex's bold cushiony body — once so amply at Uncle's disposal — without having also to listen to nonsense about the late, incomparable Noel!) as the realization that Conway never would fulfil her highest hopes. The sheer unending grit to achieve, in middle age, even a little compatibility! But there was, at least, faith to steel her will.

Faith, that other, more characteristic of her two escapes that spring. Church on Sunday mornings, the country mission — in Daniel Damascus, with Mr Mattey and his cherry-hatted daughter for company — in the evenings. (There *was* a Mrs Mattey, bound, it seemed, by inclination, to hearth and home. As for Charlotte, oh oh! for Mr Mattey had eventually confided, in a voice of deep curt shame, that she was married but had left her husband! Little Queen Cabbage, it appeared, had not tended her marriage quite as successfully as the vegetable patches of her youth!) Uncle Conway, sensing — perhaps with envy — Aunt's refuges of faith, could not resist at least one half-hearted jab of derision. 'Prayer mats in the morning, lamp oil up the nostrils in the evening. God alive, Wells, but it makes me queasy, that it does!'

'Rather, Conway, the pews of the righteous and the knee shine of the holy, than the swilling pewter pots and unpolished knees of the heathen!'

So wan she sounded, rather than defiant — for why hadn't he put his arms about her and kissed her? He did not need to say that he was sorry. Only to love.

The garage where Uncle Conway kept his car was one of the unique features of our old town house. Made of Edwardian brick, with a look forbidding as a chapel, it had formerly been a stable, its vaulted loft a storage space for hay. The loft window, long and crescent shaped, resembled, in winter, mouldy bread, a mixture of frost and whitened cobwebs; in spring and summer only the cobwebs survived. The garage below had crowded walls and corners; old tyres on nails, old coiled black rubber tubes, boxes of torn, damp leather — pieces patiently waiting their turn to be used as patches on Uncle Conway's tweed jackets ?book covers without insides, book insides without covers, and a greasy pile of motor car tools.

For me, though, the real interest was the loft. Gained by a ladder which pushed up through a large creaking wooden flap, it was barred territory — for scrambling from the ladder into the loft and from the loft back onto the ladder was, without help, impossible. Sometimes, mounting in fitful crawls, hands clinging, I'd reach the opening, then — head only half way through — peer swiftly about before a quick relieved descent. Not that there was ever anything new, chiefly old beekeeping equipment; straw hat with veil, hive frames, honeycombs, a bee smoker still stuffed with ready-to-smoulder corrugated paper. And, barbed by a thousand ancient stings! thick yellow gloves. Uncle, sitting on a plain, rickety old chair near the open flap, no more than tolerated my occasional peepings. The loft was his domain, as much his as the study to which he so often retired. Even Sam, whose curiosity was as long as his nose, skirted the garage warily.

One Saturday evening, with Sam and Mrs Hampton long gone home, and Aunt Wells out visiting a friend, I heard, from the garage, the most ferocious panting. Puzzled, I edged to the threshold. As usual, the car partly blocked the way. It had not, I thought, touching the bonnet, been used since that morning, when Uncle had arrived home smelling tipsily and late for lunch. 'Oh hurry, Conway,' Aunt Wells had called from the porch as, taking longer than usual, he'd struggled with the garage padlock. 'Our lamb will be ruined.'

'Lamb? You mean mutton,' Uncle had mumbled. Stooping, he'd squinted at the padlock from no more than an inch away. 'Catch you, with your tender heart, buying lamb!' Then, louder, 'Coming, my dear. Mutton ho!' but he'd carried on squinting and fiddling. As if he wanted to make absolutely sure that the padlock could not fly apart.

'Are you looking for dust, Uncle Conway?' I'd asked.

'Dust, boy? What nonsense. Just fixing the damn thing properly, that's all.'

'Why, Uncle Conway?'

But Uncle, apparently satisfied at last, had merely straightened up, clapped me on the shoulder, and blithely steered me towards the house. 'Mutton, Gordon, mutton. Mustn't keep mutton waiting, not the thing to do. What, Gordon, mustn't we do?'

'Keep mutton waiting, Uncle Conway.'

'Excellent, boy, excellent. You're a chip off the old block all right, even if I'm not your father. What are you?'

'A chip off the old block, Uncle Conway.'

But now, as I crept round the car, I began to wonder. All that fuss with the padlock! Had Uncle brought something home that morning, in his car? Something secret?

Emerging round the rear of the car I saw that the loft flap was open with the ladder, removed from its big supporting nails on the garage wall, angled upwards like a stack of grey-rimmed squares. Near the top of these squares Uncle's gleaming black shoes, short pin-striped legs, and small, tightly shining rump. His whole lower portion writhing with exertion he was emitting gigantic gasps. Evidently he had wrestled something of considerable size and weight up the ladder and now, exhausted, was pushing whatever the object was onto and along the loft floor, just out of sight. 'Bloated kippers in November,' he breathed out jerkily. 'My Sainted Aunt in July! Hollyhocks in April!'

'Uncle,' I called out. 'What are you doing?'

Everything wobbled, legs, rump, shoes. Then round and down, out of the loft, came Uncle's face, red, peering, eyes like huge boiled sweets.

'You, Gordon! Damnation, boy! Creeping about like a blasted Red Indian. What are *you* doing?'

'Watching you, Uncle Conway,' I said. 'And listening. You're puffing like a hippopotamus!'

Down the ladder, stumbling and bouncing, Uncle came. At the bottom, without waiting to mop his steaming face, he disengaged the ladder, hefted it back onto its place on the wall, then, with a pole, lowered the rumbling wooden flap. All with much gusty blowing. Then, free at last to mop his face, Uncle collapsed onto a large rattling box full of old medicine bottles.

'You need a bath, Uncle Conway,' I said sternly. 'Aunt Wells had one just before going out. She said she wanted to baptise herself in the cool refreshing lake of Adam's ale.'

Uncle, still mopping, said nothing; his eyes, swivelling upwards towards the loft, may or may not have been visualising Aunt Wells in her bath. If not, what a pity! for it must have been a fair and wondrous sight, Aunt Wells rising naked from her cool refreshing waters, erect, slim, pale as her damp slight breasts — Enchanting enough for Uncle Conway to have caught and held as, with graceful legs and extended arm, she stepped over the hard unfeeling bath rim? One of her hands picking up and holding, about her middle, a towel of ... yellow? Until Uncle Conway, very gently, removed the towel — Was there such a time, tender, exciting, long before shyness, uncertainty, before all the clogging awkward dust of married years was allowed to settle, multiply? When it should, by brooms of twin desire, have been swept away and lost.

'What was it, Uncle Conway?' I said abruptly, sitting down

near him on a box. 'What were you dragging up the ladder? What is it you've put in the loft? A — a box of ammunition for killing Reds and Socks? Another gun?'

But Uncle didn't answer. Instead, with a sudden change of mood, a return of the old ebullience, he leapt to his feet, holding out, low to his one side, the damp wrinkled handkerchief with which he'd been mopping his brow.

'Come on, boy. Let's make some practical use of that inquisitive head of yours. You be the bull. Charge, charge!' Then, as I stared in bewilderment, 'Charge your Uncle Conway, the finest matador in all Spain!'

11

The voices of a sunlit springtime evening. The strains of the post-benediction hymn. (Sun of my soul, Thou Saviour dear, It is not night if Thou be near). The harmonium coaxing the last gentle surge, the last offering of song. Only a little room, its walls panels of lightly coloured oak, framed by squares of rougher, darker wood. At each end a window half of plain glass, half of coloured; one window behind the congregation, one behind the lectern. On the preacher's right hand the little harmonium, on his left the door to a tiny store-room. Each bench holding no more than five worshippers. A crescent of coloured glass over the door, with Welcome in grey lead lettering. Inside, unlit this fine evening, the two oil lamps of black and gold and white — fat stately ladies immaculately dressed for the theatre! opulent as a painting by Renoir. I was seeing Aunt's new joy and solace — the little country mission.

It had all come about quite unexpectedly. Uncle Conway, rather heavily donning angel's wings, had stepped jauntily up behind Aunt Wells, gripped her by the arms and said, gruffly, 'It's time I did my good deed. Time I gave you a little treat.'

Aunt, surprised, had let him kiss her. Then, abruptly, 'Yes,

Conway, what is it? What do you want?' She sounded tired, lean and slack as her silken sleeves.

'I'd like to drive you to the mission on Sunday, that's what,' Uncle breezed. 'Damn Hall Mattey! My wife in that old tub of a car! Outrageous!'

Aunt Wells caught her breath. Conway accompany her to the mission? Conway sit beside her on a low brown bench, his knees together, his trousers rubbing on the gruff old wood? Conway mumbling the Lord's Prayer, roaring hymns? Fantasy! Impossible! Yet, was it? A smile began to light Aunt's face. Perhaps, for an instant, she saw a new marriage, a new start. Their kisses blessed and deepened and made absolutely right by the kiss of heaven.

'No God-cringing, boot-licking ritual for me, of course,' Uncle Conway said. 'I'll park up the lane, then go a stroll while you're inside absorbing those badly plotted, Biblical fairy tales of yours. All that fresh country air should do me good. Might even find an inn.' Then, as though, despite his sudden breezy good-nature, he found a further taunt at Aunt's beliefs quite irresistable, 'And don't forget to salve your lips for Sunday. So they won't be chafed too much from kissing His invisible hem! I am correct, am I not? Your Jesus does wear skirts?'

'No, Uncle Conway,' I intervened, secretly relishing Aunt's shocked face, 'a red robe. For fighting in Spain!'

On Sunday, the drive into the country. The air warm with spring. The quiet lanes, the banks of thickening green with their knops of shining yellow. Near the mission Uncle parked by a gate then went rolling off, hat cockily aslant, cigarette puffing. Inside the mission Aunt and I sat near the back while, ramblingly, the little congregation gathered: Mr Marley, an elderly farmer; Mrs Rollins, a lady with fascinating, blue veined elbows; several middle-aged couples; a little knock-kneed man — Mr Raven, Aunt called him — and the local policeman, a dour faced gentleman called Sidney. A lady whose thick eyebrows appeared to shine with grease, gave out hymn books. There were also two young girls with protuberant teeth who kept turning and grinning at me. A shuffle and scraping on the metal mat outside the door and in from the balmy sunlight, his bicycle left leaning perilously in everybody's way, came Mr Edgar in his best dingy black, pausing to grasp Aunt's hands and whisper, 'A beautiful evening, to be sure.' And then, gazing at me, 'Well done, young man!' Just as if, by appearing at the mission, I'd suddenly become a goody-goody! The harmonium was the next to sound, grudgingly, roughly shimmering under Mr Edgar's slow meek fingers (where was Betty? but then, there wasn't room for two on Mr Edgar's old bike!) Mr Mattey, too, making his entrance — silver watch in hand, limbs still stiff from Daniel Damascus! Quietly jovial all the same, pausing to lean across Aunt Wells and address himself to me. 'No loaves today? No basket? But it's in the mind, isn't it, young ferret? The real nourishment, the real good that needs to be multiplied.' And Aunt Wells, looking at me, suddenly and fully smiling for the first time that day. 'He has been to morning church,' she said, almost archly, 'so he ought to be full of good thoughts. We must hope so, anyway.'

'Indeed yes, dear madam. A veritable bundle of possibilities, I'm certain!'

When the service began Mr Mattey, occupying a bench on the other side, wasn't the preacher; instead, with his fashionably dressed daughter beside him, he contented himself with as many fervent holy ejaculations as his shaggy thistly grey throat could manage. But holy murmurings abounded, even Mr Edgar, crouched over his harmonium, dewy pear shaped nose practically bumping one of the black key stops, uttered, during one particularly boring prayer — so long it made me itch — several heartfelt Amens. To be expected, I thought. Sissy little man! Beside me, as if aware of my impiety, Aunt stirred uneasily, her white gloves pointing sharply upwards. Midway through the sermon, something made me turn my head. There, outside, looking in through the rear window, with his head turned almost upside down (he was, I think, balanced on a grassy bank, and must have been supporting himself by pressing stubby arms against the building) was Uncle Conway! His eyes, bulging with effort, strain and water, appeared to be staring not at myself or Aunt, or even at the congregation in general, but at Mr Mattey's daughter, Charlotte, as — serenely unaware under her big, floppy, cherry hat of being stared at — she sat gazing dutifully at the preacher.

Voices from one of the rooms off the hall made me stop and listen and scratch my knee. 'I have never been abroad, even to Scotland,' I could hear Mr Edgar saying. 'Though they tell me the burns are delightful. Yes indeed, splashy and bright, a tonic

70

to the toes.' 'Catch me paddling in brooks and rivers!' came the bold fretful voice of Auntie Alex. 'Too much respect for the old ankles. Fattens the marrow and weakens the bone, does water. Ankles should be dipped in good honest Scotch whisky, or not at all!'

A long pause, following which the voice, somewhat weaker than usual, of Aunt Wells.

'Will everyone have another cup of tea? Mr Edgar?'

Slipping off my satchel and kicking it into the hall stand among the dusty brassy feet of a dozen sticks and umbrellas — the umbrellas like broken, petrified bats, the sticks clattering — I rushed exuberantly into the little room where Aunt stood serving, from a tall polished wagon, tea and squashy, cream laden cake.

'I'll have a cup!' I cried. 'My belly's ever so dry! Lots and lots of sugar, please, Aunt Wells!'

She was sitting on the settee, beside her mother. A red bandeau brightening her brown pretty hair. Baskets, loaves and fishes, I thought. Coffee cream! A sudden, embarrassed watering in my nose, I gazed down at the carpet. The rich pile of yellow and magenta — with its repetitive pattern of wavy lines — was suddenly a dusty foreign landscape, full of imaginary hills and deserts. How I wished that I could ride away over that clean fluffy dust, traversing the mellow lines. Journeying for ever on a dark plodding mule! But the carpet, suddenly watery, traitorous as my nose, contracted, became one colour, became a shimmering yellow towel!

'Why, it's young squeaker,' Betty said. 'How are you, pet?'

Unable to answer, I was vaguely aware of a slender arm stretching out, taking tea and cake from Aunt Wells. With a face like fire I raised my head — obviously I couldn't stare at the carpet for ever — and looked for refuge at Mr Edgar, sitting uneasily nearby in a buxom old armchair, his dark hair a trifle matted and shiny, as if, under ordeal, perspiration was exuding unrestrainedly. Definitely he seemed nervous, tapping out piano notes on one dusty knee, balancing, with a slight quiver, his tea cup on the other dusty knee. Auntie Alex, by lusty contrast, looked far from nervous — perhaps indeed she was the only one present not suffering from apprehensions. Flapping restlessly and excitedly, with plump hands, at the reef of softly jagged cushions rising all about her, she was like a friendly seal, barking, entertaining, quite reckless as she twitched and cavorted.

'He's always,' she said, winking at me, 'thinking of his belly, as boys should. Isn't that so, Wells? Always thinking of his belly. The cute little man!'

Aunt Wells, these days wearing a smile as fixed and formal as the pattern on her Worcester china tea cups, nodded quickly and took a deep yet genteel bite of creamy cake. After which, elegant lips unmarked by the slightest trace of that rich delight, 'You may help yourself, Gordon, to a slice of cake. And cup of tea.'

Quite bereft of appetite, still hot and embarrassed, I turned my back, squinting along the wagon. My nose was running and I hadn't a handkerchief.

'As I was saying,' Auntie Alex said, jerking her thumb at Betty and Mr Edgar, 'these two should come and live with me. Why not? Plenty of room at Belle Lilac. Suppose I did accidentally see George without his trousers on? Belle Lilac's dark enough to hide his blushes, and his vitals. And I don't. Blush, that is. Gave that up when I married Noel. He wasn't always wearing trousers. My God no!'

Did God wear trousers, all the time, I wondered suddenly? Or, like the late Mr Hallet, occasionally go without?

'In fact, before Betty was born, he often sat around in combinations, especially when composing poetry in the summer. Just thinking it all out in his head, lovely phrases — born of the sun, you might say, minted out of August bank holiday gold. If there was bank holidays then, which I doubt. Oh yes, one of nature's poets. Just as he was always one of nature's gentlemen, even without his trousers on. My God though, that Spanish Franco! Suppose *he* sits in his summer combinations, reciting and composing verses? Be significant, that. A proof of my beloved Noel living again in resurrection. Oh, Betty thinks I'm daft, don't you, Betty?'

'Yes, mother, I do,' Betty said, sounding brisk and tense. 'I think you talk wildly. I always seem to be apologising for the way you talk.'

'Scotland,' said little Mr Edgar, hopefully, 'yes, we really must go there. The border country, particularly delightful, I'm told. Small old watchtowers, kestrels and fat trout. A paradise, to be sure.'

'They haven't even a bathroom with a proper bath,' said Auntie Alex, sniffing. She stirred her tea, vigorously.

'Disgraceful, that! You wouldn't think the prime minister would allow it.'

'Gordon, do sit down and eat your cake properly, over a plate,' Aunt Wells snapped. 'Dropping crumbs all over the wagon! Really, I despair of the boy.' Shockingly, a smear of cream showed on her finely drawn mouth.

'Blessed if I'd put up with just a bit of old zinc,' Auntie said. 'Even if I could get my amples into it, which is doubtful. Never was more unwashed, my glories more unwholesome, than when I stayed with these two!'

Sitting in a chair facing Betty, clutching tea, I felt my cake-filled plate grow dewy, ice-cold on my knees.

'And why I blame the prime minister is, he could order better building,' Auntie said. 'Oh George's little house was built years ago — under that beastly old ram, Dave Lloyd George, I shouldn't wonder — but they're all the same, these premiers. All tarred with the same brush. What we really need is a general. An army man. At number ten. Get things done, would an army man. Oh lordy, I'm back to Franco, aren't I? Bet *he* doesn't wash in a zinc bath. Wouldn't magnetize his vitals with zinc, that I daresay!'

'Mother, honestly! George, speak to her!'

'What's all the fuss?' Auntie Alex grumbled. 'Wells is like me, ain't she? A woman of the world. Blimey, when I think of a lovely young couple like Betty here, and George, and not a bathroom between them ... ' She stopped momentarily, and I felt her eyes, as if they were playing some wretched game of musical chairs, also stop, dead on me! 'And what do you say, little man? Agree with your old auntie, do you? I bet you've a lovely bath, hot water geyser and all, eh, son?'

My nose, surely, was about to drip, horribly and publicly, into my tea cup! 'Yes,' I mumbled into the waiting silence, nostrils clenched, head bowed. 'Hot — hot water!'

'As it should be for everyone. Geysers and hot water galore!' Auntie said. 'And especially for newly weds, loving in health and perspiration. Till death,' she ended extravagantly, and perhaps, a trifle wistfully, 'do them part!'

Oh what was Betty thinking? If only I could have known! It might have been some comfort while staring miserably at the carpet, knees damp, hands damp, nose wet and tortured beyond endurance. Was she thinking of our secret, that moment when, turning unsuspectingly around from the despised zinc bath, she had seen me rooted, gazing? Wide-eyed, seeing so much more of her than I had ever seen before. Did she pity my blushes, did she understand? Such a secret! Or was I wrong? Was it our secret only in my mind? Had she told Mr Edgar about it? And was that why he was looking at me now with mournful eyes that looked as dark as Aunt Wells' freckles? Did he know? Could I be sure of anything, anyone? Only of Aunt Wells, I thought. For sure she didn't know. And I hoped, oh how I hoped, that she never would.

'Aunt Wells,' I mumbled abruptly. 'May — may I be excused?'

'Yes, Gordon, certainly you may,' Aunt said, probably with relief. 'Off you go. And don't hinder Sam.'

But before I reached the door, before I'd even passed the settee, a bare arm had swept out, halting, delaying. In my ear, Betty's sweetly warm breath.

'Gordon, I meant to tell you. That little owl. The man I took him to was able to make him better. Isn't that splendid? I expect he's back in the trees now, hooting at night, and eating mice.'

'Mice,' moaned Auntie Alex. 'Don't, Betty. Mice! Oh my God!'

Of course. The little owl. I had nearly forgotten. It was Betty's small naked breasts that I had chiefly remembered and thought about, not the owl.

There was something else that I had remembered and thought about, too. Something that, with Betty's white fragrant arm still gently holding me, I wanted with all my heart and soul.

12

It wasn't easy, digging at heavy clay with a spade almost my own height. After only five minutes I stopped, glaring round me at the dry hard valleys and old vegetable roots of Belle Lilac's plain front garden. Gosh, I thought, Sam's right, turning over the a-soil is blooming sweaty! All the same, there was a certain malicious satisfaction to be gained in standing saucily and lawfully in the middle of that formerly sacred territory. If only Miss Young and Miss Cuthbert could see me now! 'It's that boy again,' I could imagine Miss Young's aghast voice. 'Oh those staring eyes, and that outrageously long tongue.' And her equally vibrating companion, Miss Cuthbert, 'What is he doing to our cabbage patch with that dreadful spade? Slicing! Slicing all our darling little worms! Stop him, dear, at once!' One of them, I thought, might well be watching me in any case — the one in heaven. With that unfortunate lady in mind, 'Tally ho!' I cried, driving in the spade. 'Death to worms! Charge of the spade brigade! Boom, boom, boom!'

It was a fine Saturday afternoon with long jagged clouds streaming in the breeze. With the weather in mind — settled and cool enough for hard work — Aunt Wells had tolerated no nonsense. 'Your penance for your recent rudeness to Mrs Hallet — when you referred so disrespectfully to her chamber pot — is long overdue, Gordon,' she had said. 'Oh I don't *want* to punish you, but I will not give the impression that we tolerate, or ignore, rudeness. At a time convenient to Mrs Hallet, you will call and turn over a vegetable patch for her. That time is now. You will go at once to Belle Lilac, taking with you an appropriate spade. You are, I think, old enough and strong enough, for such an exercise.'

'I don't want to go and dig up rotten old turnips and things, Aunt Wells. Make Sam go!'

The sun playing on Aunt Wells through the library window

shrank suddenly to the shape of a small golden rose on the peak of her hair. If it were a real flower, I thought irately, I'd snatch it, tug off its petals! Or dash it to the ground! Or seize a watering can and give Aunt Wells, and her rose, a real soaking!

'No, Gordon, I will not make Sam go. Nor is this matter open to further discussion.'

I looked sideways at the nearby table, at the little suede book of love poems never far these days from Aunt's hand, at daffodils in a vase. And now the rose across Aunt's hair fled with fragile speed as a curious, early afternoon gloom filled the room, engulfing all the corners.

'One thing, Gordon, puzzles me greatly. Mrs Hallet, when she called the other morning, made a reference to — '

For sure Aunt was about to say something terrible. She sat hesitating. Strangely embarrassed, freckled thumbs worrying in her lap, cuffs rubbing against slender nervous wrists, plain trim nails moving, glistening. Suddenly my heart crashed, my ribs began to ache. Without daring to move, I kept looking at the door. It wasn't far but Aunt was closer. Commandingly so.

'A reference to the — the whiteness of her body.' Aunt Wells, as she usually did when discomfited, looked at the ceiling. 'As if you had seen it!'

My throat, irretrievably huge in that moment, seemed slowly, painfully to swallow the rest of my body. Eyes, eyelids, back of the neck, my slippery palms as they clutched each other behind my back, even my scoured, indigestible kneecaps —

'*Have* you seen Mrs Hallet undressed, Gordon?'

I wanted the sun back, a golden rose shining in my eyes. Obliterating all the guilt I knew was there.

'Well, Gordon?'

'Y-yes, Aunt Wells. Once — once when I called at the public house. Only some of her though. The — the top part. Not all of her, I swear!'

But I had seen all of Betty, well, except for the part that little towel had hidden! Quivering, I fixed my muzzy gaze on Aunt's bleakly shining cuffs. Definitely definitely, that was something that she must never know!

'It's not, Gordon, a matter for embarrassment,' Aunt Wells said, surprisingly perhaps in view of her own evident shyness. 'If you saw Mrs Hallet accidentally that is that. Although it was, I suspect, all a result of your reprehensible habit of not knocking

76

on doors.' She paused, a wry little smile pulling at her mouth. That I should follow — if only with my eyes — in Uncle's errant steps! 'We'll say no more about it.' Tiredly, as if trying to tap away endless harassment, Aunt tapped her nose. 'Off to Belle Lilac, then.'

There was, though, one more question as I passed her.

'Where is your Uncle Conway?'

'I don't know, Aunt Wells. I haven't seen him since I saw him in the garden after dinner. Kicking stones and singing!'

These days Uncle Conway always seemed missing, though perhaps he wasn't all that far away. The signs were there; the door of the garage open, the car halfway out, and behind the car the tall grey ladder locked in position. Was that where he was? In the loft? Singing, drinking from his little flask, dozing in that rickety old chair? Perhaps trying on the bee keeping equipment, shambling about the creaking loft in great thick gloves, straw hat and veil! Attempting, from time to time, to set fire to himself with the bee smoker! Or was there something else that he did up there? Something appalling and furtive that Aunt Wells must not know about? But, hard though I tried, I could not think what this terrible thing might be.

'I bet he talks to himself, though,' I said aloud, scooping up earth and stones on the dull grey face of the spade. 'I bet he says death to the Reds! Just like I say death to the worms!'

'What, talking to yourself, little man? Whatever next!' And Auntie Alex, an affable smile bending the fat moist corners of her scarlet mouth, teetered studiously across the furrowed earth. In her hands a tall glass of ginger beer, its foam just like her décolletage — a gleaming, bubbly frill.

'Gosh, thanks!' I said.

Maybe, after all, Auntie Alex wasn't so bad! Even that weird black beauty spot on her brow looked a little less strange as, in five huge swallows, I drank the ginger beer. Warily, unable to judge for sure her present mood, I handed back the glass.

'That's it, you drink it all in one gulp,' she said approvingly, standing on tiptoe and peering deep into the froth lined glass, then whipping it about in a circular motion as if to be certain of its emptiness. 'That's what boys were given Adam's apples for! To swallow ginger beer in one big gulp.'

'Not one,' I said, indignantly. 'More than one. You weren't counting properly!'

Auntie's dress, neckline excepted, was a storm splash of mustard coloured polka dots, with tiny cap sleeves that left her plump arms bare for most of their faintly pebbled, faintly purple length. As usual, too, much volcanic bare chest, though this time, perhaps in deference to the spring wind, a tiny, puritanical white handkerchief poked up in the centre of that outrageous décolletage. Seeing me staring Auntie at once seized the handkerchief by its embroidered edge and drew it out. 'Pretty ain't it, son? Had it years. Only wear it to keep the chill out. And be respectable when the vicar calls. Well, holy church! Mustn't give holy church the naughty-fever, the urge for immortal sin — so to blasphemously speak — must we?' She paused, resting a pale thumb companionably against my neck. 'No need to be respectable for you though, is there, little man? Seen it all, and loved it too!'

Somehow, I wasn't embarrassed. I knew by now how tremendously proud Auntie Alex was of her breasts. Interesting, though, that every time she mentioned them her breath had that warm, raw, almost violent odour. Flasks and bottles, I thought, made wise by my long experience of Uncle Conway, bottles and flasks!

Thinking it might please her, and bravely ignoring the jet of highly aromatic air all down my neck, I nodded fiercely several times. It worked.

'That's my little fruit cake! Want another glimpse, do you? Here, take a look,' and she bent forward so that her dress pinched flamboyantly out. 'Gorgeous, eh? Tit hills incomparable. As my Noel used to say before he died and became a Spanish general, a risen Franco, so to speak.'

'Yes,' I said, peering into the rustling, frilly cavity, sighting breasts huddled like bleached fat lemons in the champagne coloured packing of the dress. 'They are indeed, Auntie Alex. The best in the world!'

Peculiar thoughts were running through my mind, an idea so ambitious that it took my breath away. Though why not? The more I thought about it the better it seemed. After all, Auntie Alex emphatically wasn't so bad. She had brought me ginger beer. She had voluntarily shown me her prized tit hills. Not long ago she had kissed and embraced me. She *must* like me. Added to that, wasn't I working for her, digging up her rotten old vegetable patch? (Quite forgotten, as excitement churned within me, that the digging was a punishment!) Only, how to mention it? How to ask her? Come to think of it, there was no one else I could ask. Betty wouldn't do — oh heavens no! — or Mr Edgar. Perhaps Mr Edgar least of all.

'That commode which Aunt Wells gave you. The one with the raspberry coloured cushion,' I said, abruptly. 'Have you sat on it yet, Auntie Alex?'

The raw breath suddenly retreated to far above my head. The pressure on my neck vanished as Auntie's thumb fell to her side.

'God, whatever next? My Noel must be stirring under his chippings! Have — have I sat on the commode?'

'Yes,' I said quickly. 'Is it all right? Have you tried it?'

'Oh lordy!' Auntie said. 'Oh my God! Tried it? Oh Noel my beloved, are you shuddering there below? Are you turning on your side? Are the ribs of your skeletal banging in the dark? I've never heard the like. Not even Betty spoke so frank, not at your age, son. Or asked so personal a question. If Noel's abroad, he'll be across the water like a shot. Dropping his Spanish battles, his Spanish war, to do a gallant for his Alex. Ever had your bum tanned, son? By a general? Oh, my navy blue!'

'Please, Auntie Alex,' I said, stubbornly. 'The commode. Is it all right?'

'Well,' said Auntie, changing suddenly around, her thick spiky lashes abruptly youthful and dancing. 'I guess it is all right! Least it takes my weight. A snug fit. Important that, when you're sitting!'

'You didn't pay for it, did you?' I said accusingly. 'Aunt Wells gave it to you for nothing!'

'Yes, as a matter of fact she did. Bountiful, I'll say that for her. Wouldn't take a single copper for her purse.'

I took a breath so deep it seemed to lift my trousers. My whole face, as I stared guiltily down at the spade, felt puffed and feverish.

'You haven't given us anything, though, have you? And I gave you that magazine! The one with the picture you liked! Uncle Conway said he'd wondered where it had got to. But I gave it you!'

Auntie Alex, gazing now in bewilderment, said nothing. She could, perhaps, have mentioned the little poetry book, but I doubt if it occurred to her. The reek of her breath came strongly, in spasms on the wind.

79

'It — it doesn't matter about Aunt Wells. Or Uncle Conway. They've got enough,' I said, 'But you could give *me* something.'

'Is that so, little man. And what, pray, can I give to you?'

'A — a mermaid, that's what I'd like! A little china mermaid! Uncle Conway has a china lady with an urn on her head. In the hall. I don't want that! I want a china mermaid. Because,' I added, writhing inwardly yet somehow inspired to a desperate courage, 'I'll be swimming soon. Aunt Wells says I can have lessons. In a year or two. So — so I want to collect china fish. And mermaids. That's — that's what I want to do.'

Breeze wafted over the bleak garden. My shoe, as if it didn't belong to me, rubbed against the steel of the spade. A robin hopped on the dark disturbed earth.

'Oh my God,' said Auntie Alex at last. 'You've seen that little thing they've got at Betty's, haven't you? On their bedroom window ledge. Well I'm jiggered!' Floundering, plainly amazed, she didn't seem able to stop staring at me. 'God, whatever next!'

'May I have it? Or one the same,' I said. 'Only, don't tell Aunt Wells. She'll only say I'll break it. And I won't, Auntie Alex, honestly. I'll take ever such good care of it. And Aunt Wells, why, Aunt Wells need never know!'

13

'You could buy it off Betty,' I said, 'and give it to me! Nobody would ever know, would they, Auntie Alex? Not even Betty.'

Suddenly confidence was oozing from me; if there were flaws in my little plan they had yet to appear. Spade forsaken — riveted in the ground, it leant slightly towards us like a curious old man — I gazed brightly and trustingly up at the beetle-black beauty spot, curly hair, and freshly post-luncheon rouged cheeks of my new friend. At that moment Auntie Alex seemed as big and strong as Belle Lilac; straddling the bumpy earth she seemed to touch

80

the sky, reassuringly solid against the flowing cloud behind her. There were, though, the mounting signs of unreliability; the slightly wobbly knees, the tumbler — along with the tiny handkerchief, crumpled now — held so carefully in both hands, the slightly dragged breath as if the body couldn't quite cope. And, above all, the alternately concentrated, then slowly wandering, gaze. As angrily shining, as persistently flinty, as the bevelled edge of the tumbler, it moved studiedly to and fro, down to my knees, then up again. Settling, finally, between my eyes, plummeting on the bridge of my nose. Despite my exertions a splendidly dry nose this afternoon — so dry in fact that the nostrils felt scratchy, as if full of fluff. Somehow the sensation in my nostrils linked suddenly with Auntie's feet. She was wearing her slippers, I realised, looking down — the fat pink slippers with those soft round garishly white tassels. Was the inside of my nose a bit like that? Woolly, dusty balls? If so I'd have to get a handkerchief, blow them out! Would Auntie lend me hers? Aunt Wells always said never use handkerchiefs belonging to other people, and never never pick a strange one up. 'A discarded handkerchief, Gordon, is like a gift from the Greeks. One must beware.' But Auntie's hanky was surely clean? Freshly plucked from the large, soft cradle of her white chests. What harm? But then I looked and saw that it was no longer merely crumpled; with a slow clumsy movement of one hand she had stuffed it into the tumbler and was twisting it round and round, not smoothly but in fits and starts.

'You shouldn't have done that, Auntie Alex,' I said indignantly. 'I wanted to blow my nose. It might have fluff balls in it!' And I looked sternly back down at her slippers. They, too, were now moving in fits and starts; flat though they were they seemed inadequate to still her wobble, anchor her properly to the ground.

'Well I'm jiggered,' Auntie said again, just as if all those minutes hadn't passed. She twisted her neck, looking at the sky. 'A mermaid! A little china mermaid!'

'Yes,' I said, glad to return to business. 'Will you get it for me, Auntie Alex?'

Back came Auntie's eyes, lacerating into mine.

'What a nasty little fellow,' she said, sharply. 'What a nasty itching little fellow, as my Noel — beloved Franco as now is — once said when he caught a peeping Tom!'

Puzzled, suddenly uneasy, I took a step away, to the other side of the spade.

'That's men though, ain't it, son? Always wanting a handful or an eyeful. And, if they can't get it, they'll slobber over statues. Blimey though, but you're starting young!' She paused, breath hard and gusty as the breeze. 'How will it end, that's what I want to know.'

'I only want a mermaid, Auntie Alex. Only — only a mermaid.'

'That time at the sea,' Auntie said. 'Was undressing in a booth. A high class bathing booth. Paid for me to change in it, Noel my rightful lawful had. And there was this little fellow on the other side, peering through a crack. Little ginger moustache, dripping wet eyes, big dented hat with a huge black stain on it. Oh lordy, did Noel kick him! A real flying thump in the back bellows! Seems the wet-eyed little fellow made the hole himself. Wandering around — putting spy holes in bathing booths! All night long! Woodworm pest, my Noel called him. Peep grub, and not a gentleman! Back in 1921 was this, a year before my darling —'

Her voice choked off, tears filled her eyes, and there was a sudden crack as, under her retrospectively writhing hands, the tumbler broke.

'And you,' she said, not even noticing, although a streak of red, savagely bright, appeared suddenly across her fingers. 'Wanting china mermaids. Wanting to stroke their little fishy tails, maul their little china tit hills!'

'No, Auntie,' I cried, in panic. 'I — I don't want to touch it. Only look!'

But with one of those strange, lightning changes of mood, Auntie Alex was suddenly laughing. Clutching, with bloodied hands, the remnants of the tumbler — only her sticking out thumbs still pallid — swaying — at times against the wind, leaning into it, at times in tune with it so that she almost tottered and fell — she ground out laughter in hateful, breathless jabs. It was the laughter more than anything that made me turn and run. It followed me all the way across the garden, past the tall lean trees and out through the flapping gate. Like a blade tearing in my mind it accompanied me in the long rush home; up the drive, round to the side door — just avoiding Mrs Hampton's midriff as, duties discharged, carrier bag and knitting in hand, she came placidly out — all the way up the stairs, along the landing and through the door into the familiar, restful privacy of my bedroom. Only then did that pursuing laughter ebb from my mind, though not entirely, oh no, not entirely! Throwing myself face down across the purple eiderdown quilt, burying my burning cheeks in its bulging enveloping velvety chill, How I hate Auntie Alex, I thought, oh how I hate hate hate her!

Suddenly, with early evening, the breeze vanished, a sun-shower burst, and a thousand glittering tiny eyes, like the radiance of the peacock in one of Uncle's best wall prints, sparkled all across the garden. Aunt, for once oblivious of the watery beauty as it blinked and dried, sat palely in the library in her usual chair. The pages of *Emma*, one of the rare novels she fully approved of, rustling on her knees. Perhaps, sitting there, thinking of the cross her new neighbour had brought her, she felt exactly like Jane Austen's lugubrious Mr Woodhouse — indignant that life around her should have to change in even the slightest degree. Or perhaps the book wasn't really there at all, not at any rate to be looked at and properly noticed; perhaps she was totally back inside herself, remembering. *Oh love, you went to Ypres, and there you died!*

I went out into the garden. The garage was open, the car poking out. What *was* Uncle Conway up to? Stealing round I saw the ladder hooked to the raised trapdoor of the loft, and a bottle, empty, lying just under the lowest rung. Miraculously the thick glass had survived the drop, it lay like a deserted, dark green rolling pin.

Fascinated, I stood gazing up the ladder. Uncle was emphatically there. I could hear the creaking of the chair and stertorous breathing. Was he just sitting, thinking, like Aunt? My shoe, touching the bottle, felt it shudder, roll. I held my breath, expecting Uncle's blotchy face to appear. Glaring down, demanding explanations. But the chair continued peaceably to creak, the heavy breathing erratically proceeded. Fine blue cigar smoke, turning a somersault, could be seen spreading over the open space below the raised flap. Should I ascend, take one of my peeps?

Up, tortuously, I climbed, the bottle below retreating, the ladder shrinking at its base, the garage floor slanting a little as, hands shifting upwards from hold to hold, I occasionally lurched. Not far now, another rung and my hair would reach the level of the loft floor, two rungs and my eyes would look along that floor, three and head and throat would be triumphantly clear. Then, head above the boards, I was there! Three cheers, I thought, forgetting briefly how precariously I perched, how far away now the green and empty bottle. Three cheers at climbing the ladder! Three cheers for surprising Uncle Conway!

For I had surprised him. Up he struggled from the decrepit chair, eyes bulging, cigar half swallowed by small round mouth.

'God,' he gasped, choking. 'Thought for a moment, thought it was—'

And, punctured apparently in both wind and limb, back he collapsed, onto the chair. A bottle, clasped between his hands, spilled half its fluid before, upright again, being lifted hoveringly towards the already stuffed mouth. Only his eyebrows, rising like the rafters above him to a dark forbidding apex, kept their dignity.

'Why don't you help me, Uncle Conway?' I called out, suddenly alarmed. 'I can't move. I'm stuck!'

My head, drowning, bobbed and quivered in a new rich blue smoke stream. I could smell the fumes from Uncle's bottle (and another, pungent smell I couldn't place). But it was the fumes, tart, all too familiar, I chiefly noticed. Even the dark spilt patch against the boards seemed to rise, tickle my nostrils with mocking enmity. Why oh why hadn't I descended promptly? Lingering at the top of the ladder, that's what had unnerved me.

Desperately I fixed my gaze on an empty darkening bee comb. 'Help me, Uncle Conway. Help me up.'

If I was stuck, so maybe was Uncle. Slumped in his chair he didn't move. Presently, bottle between knees, cigar morosely brandished between stubby fingers, 'Thought it was your Aunt,' he mumbled. 'Your Aunt Wells. Thought — thought you were one of those damn house mops of hers, poking up to dust!'

Clinging with fierce, sticky hands I closed my eyes. Under my shoes the rung felt treacherously round and slippery.

'Help me, Uncle Conway. I — I shall fall!'

And, opening my eyes, I looked high into the rafters above.

After what seemed ages, 'Fall, Gordon?' I heard Uncle rumble. 'Damn it, boy, only angels fall. And you ain't that!'

'Angels don't fall, Uncle Conway. That isn't right. They have wings to fly with.'

Uncle, pondering the point, was silent.

'If I fall I *shall* be an angel, Uncle Conway! I shall be dead, with wings! You — you don't want that, do you?'

'God forbid, boy, God forbid.'

Stirred at last, Uncle Conway carefully placed his bottle to one side of his chair. The cigar, which by now had almost stopped smoking — judging from one last frail blue wisp — evidently puzzled him. For several agonising moments, breathing hard, he just looked at it, then, brightening, bent and thrust it into the long neck of the bottle. Instead of sticking there down it dived, into the liquor. 'Damnation,' Uncle grumbled. 'Weeds — weeds like that cost money.' And, distracted, he picked up the bottle, swirling it round and around, the dark stub of cigar helpless and leaping. Feeling dizzy I again shut my eyes. Now, though my feet were rigid, they seemed to move. Or was it the rung? I heard Uncle's voice, 'Damn it boy, the ladder's safe,' come gruffly from somewhere close. Fall, I thought, I'm going to fall, and with the thought I seemed to plunge. But I couldn't have fallen, I couldn't have moved even. For fingers gripped my arm and shoulder, hot winy breath blew into my face, and, after a moment, I was being tugged, drawn upwards, upwards and sideways, one leg and shoe suddenly jerked out onto firm loft boards, the other leg and shoe, after floundering briefly in the air, thumping down to join it. And there I lay, eyes still shut, face downwards, nose squashed on the boards, inhaling fumes as well as dust. No wonder. Presently, opening a cautious eye, I saw, a mere inch from my nose, that dark wet patch of spilt liquor. 'Ugh,' I said, shuddering upright, both eyes open, and then, squatting on my rump in the dust, staring across into that part of the loft which, unless one screwed one's head right round, could not be seen from the ladder, I saw something so amazing that my breath, imprisoned by shock, leapt and swam in my throat with all the vibrancy of Uncle's berserk, bottled cigar stub, before, like the cigar, subsiding in dark drifting wonder.

I was looking at a house!

14

Closing my eyes on lonely nights I see it again, that sunny Spanish house. The memory of it, like roller skates and acid drops and all the other myriad, precious minutiae of childhood, securely and forever with me. Perhaps, different from memory now, starker, duller. The brave new paint of its Thirties heyday flaked and gone, the once black, pretty balcony (rickety then, vanished now?) now merely grey, the shutters, once blue as a jay's bright wing, drab, pitted with worm, the front door sagging on tarnished hinges. (Where in Spain, I speculate, would it have sat, that house of long ago? In the middle of a plain? On the crest of a hill? Or in a sedate, companionable suburb, removed from the fighting, from the boot bloated dust of tramping soldiers, of guns and bombs? No! Wrong and inappropriate! Site it where the shells fall, where it runs the risk of being battered, scorched! Its outside wreathed by tumbling smoke, its balcony flecked from ash. It is, after all, more than a house. It has a name.) And the inside? How, now, those rooms of yesterday? Are they still hollow, echoing? As if looted and raped by war's exigences? Are they still in need of cleaning? Dust laden, walls and floors turned to the same thick pallor? I hope not, I hope the owners since (oh whatever did become of it?) have kept as clean as possible that ageing melancholy interior, so that its ghosts live without squalor. (Can you exist forever, a ghost on a ghostly horse? Or maybe they're still there, those two, solid and real. Maybe they never left their lonely room. Were never plucked away.) Back to the outside, the long, flat-faced frontage. A bit like Belle Lilac really, as I recall — only with the look of Spain, the shutters and balcony, the tiny crucifix hanging on the green front door, the tiny bird cage suspended in a window, the tiny geranium pot on a ledge. And that was all. Oh, except for strange red flowers trailing on the wall! Gay outside! bleak within. Practically a shell house. Rooms (with that one exception) quite deserted, no parquet flooring or maids moving soundlessly on cloth bound feet, no old dark furniture or pictures of Our Lady — benevolent, eternally pallid — on the bedroom walls! Bedrooms with no beds! No carpets either — but that was right, that was to be expected and correctly Spanish — no tables with bright chequered cloths or dull damask cloths proud with antiquity, really absolutely nothing inside the house except, as already mentioned, for — But that I don't particularly wish to remember or think about. Well, it all seems so silly now, quite absurd. And if Uncle Conway were alive I'm sure he wouldn't want to remember either.

Not a real house, and definitely not a big house. Big enough, though, to make my eyes pop!

Jumping up, ignoring Uncle, the open wooden flap, and everything else in the loft, over I crossed, staring amazedly down at a roof top that came as high as my knees.

'A doll's house!' I exclaimed, wonderingly. 'Is it yours, Uncle Conway? Where did you get it from?'

At first, back in his chair, Uncle Conway didn't speak. Exhausted, it seemed, by the rescue, he sat heaped untidily, too puffed to lift his bottle. Then, rallying, he threw back his head, took a long, boisterous, cigar flavoured gurgle. There followed several minutes of agonised splutter, after which, recovering, calm gradually returned. His little double chins smoothed away, his eyes gazed fixedly up into the rafters.

'Where, Uncle Conway? Where's it come from?'

Without looking down from his contemplation of the rafters, 'Surprised you, have I, boy?' Uncle said.

And chuckled, fruitily.

Kneeling excitedly down, 'It's new, isn't it?' I burbled. 'It smells all new.'

'Course it does. That's the paint.' Uncle said.

And with a lordly wave — eyes still watching the rafters — he indicated a cluster of small, recently used paint pots.

'Not been easy, boy. But I've done it. By God I have!'

Touching one of the small blue wooden shutters I felt the slight, sticky tug of fresh paint. In fact the whole of the outside had been painted, it gleamed as strongly as it smelt.

'You didn't make it, did you, Uncle Conway? I can see you painted it. It looks a bit smudgy in parts.'

Down jerked Uncle's head, back came the double chins.

'Cheeky young devil,' he grumbled, leaning suddenly forward and nearly tumbling. 'Course I didn't make it. Not a carpenter, am I? But I painted it, by heaven. Right down to those red flowers on the wall. Fuchsias, they're supposed to be. And glued on those wooden pieces for shutters, and that piece of sticking out wood for a balcony floor. Ticklish that. See the tiny brackets underneath. For support.' He paused, chair rising balefully up behind him as he slid to its very edge. 'Only needs a balcony railing now and Bob's your uncle, a Spanish house!

'Yes,' I said dubiously, after a moment, 'but how do you *know*, Uncle Conway? You've never been to Spain.'

'Heard about Spain, haven't I?' Uncle blustered, flushing. 'Really, lad!'

'Will you use matchsticks for the balcony railing?' 'Matchsticks? Matchsticks?' Uncle's splutter, wild as sea spray, came half across the loft. 'No, damn it, I'll get something from Dapperings. All sorts of trinkets there. That's where I got the little flower pot, and the tiny birdcage. They're sure to have something. Miniature wrought iron railings in the toy department, I shouldn't wonder.'

'But what if they haven't, Uncle Conway?'

The chair creaked, savagely.

'Then it's a balcony without a railing, ain't it, boy? No, it'll be finished, don't you worry. I'll think of something.'

'There's a cross hanging on the front door,' I said, freshly excited. 'With Jesus on it. Did you buy that as well?'

There was a long, terrible pause.

'No option, Gordon. That's how the Spanish are. Religious to the marrow,' and Uncle, sounding sorrowful, shook embarrassedly his now useless bottle. The cigar stub, tipping darkly out, lay on the boards in a mound of swiftly congealing dust — sodden, thumb-like.

'But who's it for?' I said. 'For me, Uncle Conway?'

'Who's it for?' Uncle Conway said, putting down the empty bottle and sounding almost sober, such dark fierce satisfaction in his voice. 'Alexandra Hallet, that's who it's for. Thinks I'm clumsy, does she? Not good with my hands. Well, I'll show her!'

And with a long unbridled look of satanic pleasure, he looked appreciatively down at his squat fingers.

'For Auntie Alex,' I said, astonished. 'But — but she's grown up!'

'Not too grown up for this house, Gordon,' Uncle Conway said. 'You see, my boy, it used to be behind the bar. At the York Arms. Been there for years. A genuine old doll's house. Long since lost its original furniture I guess, but otherwise fine. There just for decoration, you might say. And handy for any oddments, receipts and so on. Alex was always putting things in it herself, if I remember. And when I went in the other day — well, why not with Alex gone — there it was! Still there, dusty as ever behind the bar and among the bottles. So I bought it. There and then. Seemed only too pleased to see it go, the new mine host. Taking up too much space for his liking.'

More astonished than ever, I looked from Uncle to the house, and back again.

'And now,' said Uncle Conway proudly, 'it's a Spanish house! The kind she covets. And don't think she won't like it, boy, because she will. I've made sure of that.' He paused, thumbs pressed into each side of his tight waistcoat, swaying a little in the chair, inordinately vain and happy, as if, at the very least, he'd created a sumptuous cathedral. 'Take a look into that room on the right. The lower one. Now, what do you see?'

I looked, then, choking with rage, slowly, unbelievingly withdrew a small leaden figure. It was cast in the form of a soldier sitting grandly astride a fine prancing plumed white horse. A toy cavalryman!

'Why, this is mine, Uncle Conway. One of my old horse soldiers!'

'Not a soldier now, Gordon,' Uncle corrected, grinning. 'A general. A general, boy. Sitting on his white horse! Now, look over the door.'

Again I looked. I hadn't noticed before, but in small lettering, painted in a crescent over the green door, was the name of the house.

'And there, Gordon, you have the core of it,' Uncle chortled, wriggling with excitement, a tiny cannonade of alcoholic indigestion blending with his creaking chair.

Over the door — solemn as a black Spanish shawl — was the name Madrid.

89

15

As it happened, House Madrid — that quaint symbol of what
Auntie Alex hoped would eventually happen to the real Madrid,
General Franco riding triumphantly in on a white horse — was
completed long before that particular Saturday evening turned to
night. It could be that I was the stimulus, that having acquired
an audience, an admirer for his handiwork, Uncle was inspired
to conquest of his final problem — the balcony. For what good
that slim, projecting, slightly askew piece of wood without the
finishing grace of iron railings, or what could pass for iron
railings? Dapperings toy department might have been able to
provide something, but Monday was a long way off. Uncle was
impatient. Testily so, as if emptying his bottles had caused an
inner itch. His inebriety subdued now to a simmer, that peculiar
brain began once more to function. It suddenly occurred to him
that I had toys other than soldiers, lots more; suddenly nothing
would keep him in the loft, he must go and see what he could
find!

I remember being left alone, my feelings as I squatted on the
boards. For with Uncle gone everything changed. The beekee-
per's veil, like a black heaped net, looked sinister. The band of
the old straw hat, also black, suddenly moved — though it might
have been a spider crawling.

Shivering, seeking refuge, I looked at the Spanish house. But
even the house made me feel uneasy, as if things stirred inside.
Perhaps they did. Perhaps unseen people glided to and fro,
through the doors and rooms. Perhaps, after all, it *was* fully
furnished, perhaps it was only that I couldn't see the beds and
chairs, the old gloomy sideboards groaning with lamps and
Madonnas, the whole tortured decorative plethora of icons and
bleeding hearts, crucifixes pinioned inside and outside doors,
stairs creaking as ageing, dark wrapped servants climbed. Things
stirring? But no, when, fearfully almost, I bent forward to look,

only the dusty empty rooms and, in that lower room, Uncle's horsed general, stiffly and forever poised. Luminous the white of the horse, its legs frozen in mid-prance, its plumed head like a splashing fountain. Tempted, I nearly snatched it out again, but I didn't! Uncle had promised me a camera. If I co-operated. If I let the hateful Auntie Alex have my toy!

'No blabbing to your Aunt either, Gordon. Though, damn it, if she can give that woman a commode — ' And Uncle's voice, back on mundane matters, his great creation temporarily forgotten, had become aggrieved and liquor washed all over again. 'You heard what I said. No blabbing to your Aunt.'

'Of course I won't sneak to Aunt, Uncle Conway. Not if I can have a camera.'

'You'll have a camera,' Uncle had pledged, lurching and squeaking down the ladder. 'World's full of pictures to be taken. We might even take a picture of the Spanish house.'

If only we had! That would have been a picture worth the taking.

Uncle returned just in time. At once, ashamed of my fears, I crossed and kicked the old straw hat and veil.

'Never mind playing football,' Uncle chided. 'Look what I found!'

I looked. 'But they're not railings, Uncle Conway. They're gates!'

'Farm gates at that,' Uncle chuckled. 'But they'll do!'

With the aid of putty and black paint, Uncle was proved right. Four of the small lead toy gates, put end to end, served effectively for the balcony front, a fifth gate, carefully snapped in half, provided side railings. Wonderful, I thought! And not just the balcony. It really was remarkable how, with a few odds and ends, Uncle had transformed that once plain facade. Not that I had seen it in its original state. But even I could imagine how dowdy it must have looked.

Unthinkingly copying little Mr Edgar's favourite phrase, 'Well done, Uncle Conway,' I said. 'Well done!'

Crouching on the station platform, between the wall of the waiting-room and a heaped-up trolley, I wondered what to do. Not easy to step bravely out and say hallo! Yet my legs were aching, my neck felt stiff — and if I didn't hurry up she might be gone! I moved slightly — my knees crackled — The gum, churning in my mouth, felt suddenly undignified; plucking it out I stuck it on a parcel. And then the face of a porter — cheeks ruddy above each end of a drooping moustache — appeared over the topmost package. An unlit pipe, curling away like a horse-tail, didn't prevent the strains of Goodnight Sweetheart from hissing like railway engine steam down to where I crouched. Gripping the trolley he pulled it from the wall, turned it briskly about, and set off, wheels grinding, boots clattering, still soulfully hissing, down the platform. Exposed, up I shot, striking the back of my head. While the Nestlé's chocolate machine stayed unmoved, I saw lights!

'Why, Gordon! For heaven's sake, pet, what are you doing here?'

And Betty, who had been sitting placidly all by herself on the long grey bench, eyes daydreaming across the empty railway lines, leant and grabbed my arm.

'I've never known such a boy,' she said, 'for appearing unexpectedly. You should have been a mole!'

Since it was a Sunday morning — the morning after discovering Uncle Conway's secret — I had expected to be in church with Aunt Wells. But Aunt had risen lethargically and, after barely tasting breakfast, redrawn her curtains and returned to bed, plagued by migraine. 'It must be the vibrations from Belle Lilac!' she had complained to Uncle. 'My eyes feel like bursting!' Uncle, sympathetic for once, had actually tucked her into bed and held, for several moments, a handkerchief soaked in eau-de-Cologne against her sickly brow. After which, exhausted, he had retired to his study and an early morning bracer from his favourite magenta, pebble-dash flask. Aunt, though, wasn't letting me off so lightly. 'Gordon,' she had instructed, lying, hair strangely and fetchingly long against a pillow of exquisite, crushed purity, 'I want you to go to church as usual. I have left, in our pew, one of my best lace handkerchiefs. It is, I trust, still there. You may, though, if you wish, leave during one of the hymns.'

'If it isn't there,' I'd said, inflamed, 'I shall call the vicar a thief! I shall search inside his dog-collar!'

'Gordon, I have a severe headache. Please go, and if the handkerchief is there, bring it safely back.'

It was ten minutes after collecting the handkerchief from the church — I left during the first prayer, noisily disrupting the sighing old ladies — that I saw him. Little Mr Edgar, pushing

92

his bicycle up the incline from the railway station. A sorrowful curve to his sombre shoulders, his black stiff hat held near the bicycle bell as he pushed, his poetically lank hair made even more unkempt by the breeze. Contemptuously I watched him mount and billow away, man and bike queerly compatible, each plain and shabbily comfortable. 'A new bicycle,' I said aloud. 'That's what Aunt Wells should have given him. Not bottled plums,' and then, leaning over the railway bridge, taking my customary look with keen eyes, I saw, sitting on one of the quiet, midday platforms, the figure of Betty! A Betty neatly and prettily parcelled for travel, in pert red hat and long, duck egg blue coat. At her feet a suitcase.

Clambering over onto the embankment I scrambled along, scuffling from the clumpy, worn railway grass down into crunchy black stubble, moving cautiously lower until down, quickly, through a flowerbed to the station. Then, darting forward, in behind the trolley.

'Come and explain,' Betty said now, leaning back again although still holding my arm. 'What on earth were you doing, hiding there?'

Hanging my head, I gazed at the cigarette burning in her hand, wishing that I could glow and burn and vanish in the red tip.

'I — I was going to spring out and surprise you!'

'Well you have surprised me,' Betty said. 'Gosh, I nearly burnt a hole in my nice new coat.'

Lifting my chin I looked resentfully at the big grey buttons, and small grey collar, of the blue coat.

'Why are you wearing a coat? It's not cold.'

'But it is, pet. At least to me. A sunny but chilly morning. The trouble with boys is that they have such meaty red blood.'

My gaze roved to the suitcase, standing ominously close to her pretty, cherry red shoes. Where was she going?

'You like red, don't you?' I said, not really thinking of her shoes, still looking at the case. 'You've got a red dress. I've seen you wearing it.'

'So I have, Gordon. And it's in the case.' She looked at me questioningly, pale brown eyebrows daintily curved. 'I expect you wonder where I'm going, don't you?'

'Yes,' I said grudgingly.

'I'm going to have a holiday. Not for long. A week maybe. I shall be staying with my Aunt Josephine in Bristol.'

An Aunt Josephine in Bristol! I looked at Betty with amazement. Suddenly she had taken on a new dimension.

'That's not the seaside,' I said at last, frowning. 'Aunt Wells says Bristol has a lot of ships, but it isn't the seaside. Not like Weston-super-Mare.'

Betty laughed. 'Your Aunt Wells is right. But it's not far from Weston, so I may go there for a blow.'

Again I eyed Betty's case. And a thought struck me.

'But it isn't summer,' I said, suspiciously. 'You can't have a holiday yet!'

'Oh yes I can. Holidays are for when we need them, Gordon. Though I must say I dislike leaving poor George to cope.'

I thought of Mr Edgar, frying-pan in one hand, bicycle clips in the other, pottering about the little house in search of bacon!

'He'll be all right,' I said. 'He can play the piano. And eat tuck all day long.'

'I expect,' said Betty, laughing, 'you could do with something to eat right now. A chocolate maybe, like the one you ate at my house. Coffee cream, wasn't it? My favourite. I was saving it for last.'

Shuffling uneasily, suddenly mildewy all over, I turned away, looking up the railway line.

'Never mind, pet. I've gone off chocolates anyway, so I don't even regret not having had it. The only thing that makes my mouth water now is watercress.'

I turned, shocked. 'Ugh, horrid!' I said, thinking of the straggly watercress — in its shallow dish a kind of gigantic bird's nest, green and mouldy — that Aunt Wells often put out, in season anyway, for tea.

Placing her cigarette to her lips Betty inhaled, made a lipsticked circle, and blew steadily out.

'Nevertheless, that's what I fancy. Must be the young shaver.'

Young shaver? I didn't understand.

Deciding to change the subject, without quite knowing why, 'I saw Mr Edgar going away,' I said. 'He was pushing his bike. Why didn't he stay to lift up your case when the train comes?'

'Really, Gordon! You are critical. George has a lot to do, more than you! And it's only a light case.'

'But Aunt Wells says that gentlemen always lift cases for ladies.

A lady must never lift a case,' I said. Although Aunt Wells often refused to let Uncle touch *her* case! But that, perhaps, was if they'd quarrelled. 'You haven't quarrelled, have you? With Mr Edgar. And — and couldn't I come with you? On holiday?'

Unexpectedly, Betty blushed. It may have been the fervour in my voice, or it may have been thoughts, secret, tender, that had more to do with Mr Edgar than with me. But if it was to do with me, was she remembering, realising at last the effect she may have had while bending over, buttocks open as a peach, to touch the steaming water? Out across the glinting rails she threw her cigarette, staring into the distance, then, turning her head — so beguiling it looked under the trim red hat, curls of light fluffy brown peeping out — said gently, and just a trifle primly, 'You wouldn't like it with my Aunt Josephine, Gordon. Too dull. Besides, I'm going to rest a lot.'

'That's silly,' I said. 'You could go and look at the ships. And go to Weston every day.'

Betty nodded, smiling.

'But you could,' I said combatively.

Far off, half buried in the breeze, the first furled hootings of an approaching train. Along the line, the signal dropped.

'The other day,' said Betty, looking gravely down into her lap, 'I discovered something about myself. Something wonderful, and important. And that's really why I'm having this little holiday. To celebrate, and to rest.'

'What do you mean?' I said. 'Celebrate what? It isn't your birthday.'

But Betty only laughed that silvery laugh, leaning quickly forward to squeeze an ear and kiss, warmly and briefly, the jutting, stormy peak of my nearer eyebrow. Besides, how could she answer? the air was suddenly full of rumble, the porter had reappeared and, anxiously stroking his moustaches, was trotting down the platform. In, wheels bright, pistons punching, came the train. Hot and smoothing-iron heavy over the already immaculate shirt front of the railway lines. The peak capped driver leaning out, and, behind him, strange and grimy, the stoker, and with them a backyard of scarlet and ebony, fire and coal; and then the carriages, their windows a rattling stream of cosiness, of tiny, glass bound worlds. And just when it seemed that nothing would ever stop, the grinding down, the hissing, ebbing steam across the platform.

'Goodbye, love,' Betty said, giving me a final peck. 'Be good now. Straight off home.'

She must have gone through an already opened carriage door, so quickly did she vanish. The case, which I had meant to try and lift, had gone also.

And then, as I frantically scanned the train, I saw her in the corridor, saucy creamy nose smudged against the window, hat brim curved from pressing the grey cold glass. Smiling and waving and, yes, winking — almost as Auntie Alex often winked. Roguishly yet fondly. And the train began to move, shuddering anew, long, quickening glides. And still I didn't leave, just stood on the platform, staring and waving until train and every scrap of smoke had dwindled, gone — leaving only the winding silver track and silence.

That afternoon, in the park — playing truant from Sunday school — I remembered the mermaid. My cheeks grew hot, my nose began to run, and a nearby lady, crossing hastily over, crammed her own dainty handkerchief suffocatingly up my nostrils. Coughing from scent, eyes watering, I sat in anguish on the grass, nose-wiping away under the stern eyes of the massive, motherly lady who, towering over me like a blue silk cloud, kept tut-tutting and wrinkling her own large nose. It had been yesterday afternoon, digging the garden, when I'd broached the matter of the mermaid to Auntie Alex — time enough for Betty to have been told. Had she known that morning? As I stood beside her in the station? At the thought not only did I blush all over but my nose, again overflowing — much to the distress of the hovering blue silk cloud — completely deluged the fragile handkerchief.

'That's enough, little boy, if you don't mind,' said the blue cloud sharply, as, still in anguish, I bit a corner of the precious handkerchief. Away it flew, soggy and twisted in her hands, a ruin to be either discarded in the nearest park basket, or taken home and washed several times over in boiling water.

Why, leaving the park, I turned towards the road where Mr Edgar lived I still don't know. I hadn't been there since that memorable occasion when Aunt Wells had taken me. Yet, quite suddenly, there I was again. Holding my breath, stalking along in the shelter of the low hedges. Not, of course, that I was scared of Mr Edgar. All *he* could do was plonk pianos and play sissy hymns on organs and push a daft old bike around. When I grew up, if I had a bicycle at all, it would be one with low, sharply curving handlebars of brightest steel. Nor would I wear the type of clothes that Mr Edgar wore, dark, dusty. I'd wear a hat with a hard curly brim — like one of Uncle Conway's — or a soft big wide grey one with curling red feather. A feather so large that pretty ladies would want to steal it. And then, promptly, I forgot all about hats and feathers and pretty ladies as — reaching the hedge outside Mr Edgar's — I looked up at the bedroom window, at its orange, fluttering curtains. The mermaid was gone.

16

If it hadn't been for Enoch Balsom and the trouble he unwittingly caused between Uncle Conway and Aunt Wells, I doubt very much whether House Madrid would ever have left the loft. No doubt it would, in time, have become part of the lumber, as entrenched as the hive frames and all the other beekeeping paraphernalia, the haven only of loft spiders with a taste for the bizarre. Uncle himself occasionally climbing the ladder, making himself comfortable with bottle and cigar, his unique and solitary handiwork an increasing solace — for didn't it prove, to Uncle Conway (as his eyes glazed over and the world turned gently rosy) if to no one else, that fingers that could so artfully devise, decorate, could surely love and thrill a lady? But events weren't to allow such fulsome prideful daydreams. Enoch Balsom saw to that. For it was Enoch that made Aunt and Uncle quarrel, and it was the quarrel that made Uncle tipsy. If he had been only a quarter in his cups, or a half, or three quarters even, nothing might have happened — the house might have stayed rooted and exotic and decaying on the boards. But Uncle wholly in his cups—

The quarrel happened at teatime on that very Sunday, a tea I was only just in time for. Luckily, despite my red cheeks, Aunt Wells asked only what I'd learnt at Sunday school. 'It's important, Gordon, that memory be tested — for who wants a depleted treasure-house? Valuables lost to the mind forever.'

97

'Illogical rumbum,' Uncle Conway muttered, reaching eagerly for the snowy thatched fruit cake, its chunky, ready cut pieces lying in dark delectable steps all across the silver stand. 'Some things are best forgotten.'

'Gordon?'

'I saw Mr Balsom,' I fabricated quickly, to divert her. 'Out walking. With yellow wax sticking from his ears!'

Putting down his slice of cake — Aunt Wells always began *her* tea with bread and butter — Uncle Conway clutched his stomach, laughing.

'Oh capital, lad, capital!'

'His ears *are* waxy, Uncle Conway. I've seen it.'

'Of course you have, my boy. So have I. And not a pretty sight.'

Aunt, turning pink, looked rigidly at her plate. Mr Balsom, who lived nearby in town square, often in late summer brought her boxes of damsons, and though Aunt had damson trees of her own she always graciously accepted, with, perhaps, an excessive praise of the small, bloom-misted bounty. Even Sam disapproved. 'A-sour,' he'd grumble. 'That's all them purple furries is.' Uncle, for once in agreement, thought Mr Balsom patronising. Especially when, in addition, roses were brought round in a huge red white and yellow flooded basket of aromatic glory — as if we hadn't roses enough! A splashing, breathtaking effulgence maybe, but to Uncle all as unwelcome as cigar stubs in wine.

'I suppose, this summer, he'll be round again. With his usual basket of thorn clippings,' Uncle said, his lightheartedness subsiding. 'I abhor the old devil's damnably impertinent gifts. What's he after? A pinch of your bottom?' And, scowling, he swallowed down the bar of fruit cake, leaving, on his plate, not a single crumb to mark its passing.

'That,' said Aunt Wells, 'is a disgusting and spiteful remark about a charming, aristocratic old gentleman.'

'Oh God,' groaned Uncle. 'Just because the damn man was born in Cheltenham you put him on a pedestal.'

'Cheltenham,' Aunt Wells remarked pensively, 'has such delightful, lingering gentility. One thinks instinctively of Victorian carriages under the trees, driving down the parade.'

'And old Balsom, a lad in knickerbockers, running beside the horses, I suppose? Damnation, it makes me sick. Cheltenham — that's all he ever talks about. That and his garden produce. One wonders where he gets his fertilizer from. Catch that old dandy out of doors, shovelling manure like the rest of us! Too high and mighty.'

'*You* never shovel horse manure, Uncle Conway.' I spoke with venom; only that winter some of the precious dark steaming gold had been deposited outside our drive. Sam, ordered to collect by Uncle Conway, had gripped his knees and complained of rheumatics. 'I ain't a-picking no dung up. Not if it was the last dung in Singapore I wouldn't. Samuel's joints is too a-creaking.' Mrs Hampton, also aware of Uncle's shifting, coldly beady eye, had bustled proudly off. That eye, coming to me, had finally found a pliant target. The torment, the shame, of a public appearance, clumsily transferring unwilling horse dung, on a shovel, from road to bucket!

'If Mr Balsom doesn't go out shovelling manure in town square,' I challenged, as Uncle Conway, abashed, made no effort to rebut my charge, 'where does he get it from? Or does he steal out at night, in the dark, to get it?'

'Gordon, eat your tea!' Aunt Wells, to judge from her face, had had quite enough of a distasteful topic. 'You too, Conway. If, that is, you've room for mere bread and butter, after all that cake.'

Slowly, Uncle Conway turned a sunset glow. 'What was that, Wells?'

'I said eat your bread and butter.'

'How dare you,' Uncle spluttered. 'How dare you reprove me as if I were the boy.'

'The staff of life should always precede the self-indulgence of luxury,' said Aunt Wells loftily. 'And cake is a luxury.'

Uncle, all sunset colour now down to his last double chin, seemed to fairly rip apart.

'Damn your tea table protocol, Wells. All damn tommy rot!'

Aunt Wells, clutching a fold of tablecloth between slender, trembling fingers, tried to remain calm.

'Less rot, as you term it, than your vulgar nonsense about Mr Balsom.'

'Damn Balsom,' roared Uncle back. 'And his damsons. And his roses. And his great damn basket.'

And, irritated beyond prudence, boiling angrily to his feet, Uncle actually thrust out his stubby arm in a defiant, heated Fascist salute.

'Beau Brummel Balsom,' he thundered, jigging fanatically up and down. 'Cheltenham Charlie! Earwig Enoch!'

Perhaps it was the salute, maybe the shouted taunts, maybe both. Suddenly everything was different. The ladies with parasols in each corner of the tablecloth, their brown and green hooped skirts falling over the table edge, seemed more than ever to be gracefully tumbling to an elegant doom. Time crept by while, engulfed by a sense of Uncle's sudden disgrace, I noticed everything before me, even a speck of black on the blue of a gold rimmed plate, a speck that, though I tried, couldn't be rubbed away — it was part of the china, immoveable.

'I'm sorry, Conway, but I shall not be letting you drive me to the country tonight,' Aunt Wells said. 'Mr Mattey will be calling to know if I require a lift. I shall take his offer. It may, in any case, be for the best. There have been complaints, from people in the nearby cottage, of a prowler in a bowler hat, constantly peering in through one of the mission windows. It seems, Conway, that even you are attracted to the rites, and solemnity, of worship!'

Putting down her serviette she rose and walked from the room.

17

'Hallo, son!' And Auntie Alex, leaning breathlessly on her front gate, cheeks puffy and purple under a valiant layer of rouge and powder, the name Belle Lilac swinging gently below her rather like the dilapidated lettering on a worn old canal barge, waved me across. A cigarette, pouting between her lips, sent a disturbing, sickly cloud floating past my nose. 'You're just the one I wanted to see. Got something for you.'

It was pure chance that Auntie had spotted me at all. After Mr Mattey had arrived in Daniel Damascus — on his own for once, no Little Queen Cabbage under floppy cherry hat — and driven Aunt away, the evening had settled to a familiar course, Uncle prowling sullenly to and fro past the old tall clocks, evidently killing time until the local hostelries were open. (Had he watched Aunt leave? Had there been a telltale blink of the venetian blinds at his study window? Had he stood there glaring down, full of spluttery contempt for the whole Sunday evening enterprise? Wondering, too — as he looked in vain for the object of his secret admiration — where Little Queen Cabbage was? Whether, perhaps, she had returned to her husband? Ready, after living with her moralistic parents, to try again?) 'Oil lamps,' I heard him mutter once. 'Oil lamps for the daft and blind! That's the mission.' I said nothing — who was I to argue? Besides, the only comment he seemed to want was from the clocks. Every time he gazed, wobbling and frowning, at one of the aged faces the flask — borne by his untiring arm — rose upwards to his mouth. When Uncle vanished I at once filled a glass with water and patrolled the thick old carpets much as he had done, only — unlike Uncle — holding up the glass in invitation for the clocks to drink from. 'Water's lovely,' I told them. 'Water won't make you drunk, honest. You'll still be able to tell the time.' Then, finally bored by their proud rosewood and mahogany encased abstinence, I turned instead to an old escape. With Uncle gone who was to stop me going out? Just a little way. Say, as far as Dolly in the field at the corner. Taking with me lump sugar from our teatime sugar bowl. Like the clocks, Dolly was company too — while the sugar lasted. After that she snuffled, flicked her tail, and headed sturdily for the far side of the field. No better than the clocks, I thought — at least they hadn't moved away! And it was cold — even I felt the chill as May sunshine stamped a bleak brief mosaic of light and shadow on the grass.

It didn't occur to me that Auntie Alex, when she called me from her gate, might have something that I wanted. The memory of our last encounter, of her fierce, upbraiding laughter, wasn't forgotten, nor could it ever be. Scuffling my shoes, wanting to sneeze and hurry on home, I glared at the vaporous cigarette. It was one of those sissy Turkish ones!

'That's a stinker you're smoking,' I said pugnaciously. 'It's making me cough.'

'Is it, little man? I'll put it out then. Anything for you!'

Unbelievingly I watched her toss down the cigarette and grind her fat fluffy slipper all over it. Slippers apart she was, perhaps, in her Sunday best — wearing a stiffly rustling cap-sleeved silvery dress with a low square black-edged neckline. It was one I hadn't seen before, the silvery part was replete with patterned clusters of oranges, and there was a wide orange coloured belt with a big black buckle round her plump middle. Her arms and throat, obviously feeling the chill, had that slightly purple, slightly dingy, pebbled look.

'Not too keen on Turkish, myself,' she said, turning back to the gate. 'My late hub, Noel, now campaigning in Spain, God bless him — lordy how that war drags on — always said Egyptian and Russian and Turkish wasn't manly tobacco at all. Fancy stuff for the harem, and the pansy brigade, he used to say.'

'But he's not really in Spain, is he, Auntie Alex?' I said, provoked. 'You showed me his grave last summer. He can't be in Spain.'

'Ah, that's the question, ain't it, son? Where's my Noel? Well, only God knows, that's what I say.'

'We seek him here, we seek him there, those Frenchies seek him everywhere. Is he in Heaven? Is he in Hell? That demned, elusive Pimpernel,' I recited proudly.

'Lovely. Lovely, son,' Auntie cackled, clapping beringed, flashing hands, and showing a gold tooth lurking to one side of her front teeth.

'That's new,' I said promptly. 'I haven't noticed that funny coloured tooth before.'

'Like it, son? It is fairly new. Here, take a proper look,' and she bent sociably over the gate, mouth wide. You smell! I thought, edging back. You've been looking at clocks and drinking!

'Come on in then,' Auntie said sharply, opening the gate. 'Didn't you hear me? I've got something for you.'

Something for me? At last it registered.

'The mermaid,' I cried, inspired. 'Have you got the mermaid for me, Auntie Alex?'

'Yes, little man, course I have. Not your Auntie for nothing am I?' And, grinning with gratification, she pressed her large colourless thumb confidentially to her lips. With one of her heavy black-lashed eyes closing and opening in an attempted wink, she had rarely looked more weird. But, in that instant, I thought her at least an angel.

'Not a word, neither, about why I wanted it. Just told Betty, last night, I fancied it and over she handed it, like a lamb. Never even breathed your name. Just the way you asked me, son — utter secrecy.' Her thumb, sliding and pulling on the garish surface of her full lower lip, slid suddenly right off, her arm falling jerkily to her side. 'Aren't you pleased, little man? Aren't you pleased your Auntie's got you the mermaid?'

'Oh yes, Auntie Alex. Of course I am!'

'Then come on in. Oh lordy, this gate! Be falling apart one of these days.'

As we moved past the thin trees and along the path, her right hand bearing solidly on my shoulder, 'You never finished digging that patch, son,' she admonished. 'Won't do, won't do at all. Suppose my Spanish general came to call, and all that rough ground with not even a new cabbage to bless it and make it green?'

'Gosh, Auntie Alex, is a general really going to call on you?'

'When he's won the war, son, when he's won the war. When he's ridden into Madrid on his white horse and waved his big plumed hat and thrown kisses to all the ladies.'

'They'll be on balconies, won't they?' I said eagerly. 'The ladies. Throwing flowers! I've read of ladies throwing flowers from balconies.'

'You're a clever little lad,' said Auntie Alex, pausing to breathe heavily and look me over, ruffling, with her heavy hand, my already well threshed hair. 'God though, he's like my Noel, that Franco. Uncanny, it is. Makes my tit hills rise like toadstools in the night. If I stop and think about it.'

We had come to the front door of Belle Lilac. Auntie, after beckoning me into the porch beside her, began to writhe and fumble. Plunging an extraordinarily puffy hand into her bosom she seemed to be searching for the loop of an unfamiliar, tatty string that hung round her neck. 'Sometimes put my front door key here,' she said, grunting and blowing with endeavour. 'No better place, eh, son? No more privileged metal in all the world than this key. Next to my skin, bless its impudence! Lying like a silver brook between the high Northumbrian hills of my milky bouncers — as my Noel once said when I wore a neck charm he bought me. On honeymoon we were, up North and actually paddling in a brook. Well, I was young then. And this charm cold as water round my neck and between my lovelies. Oh I wish I could remember all he used to say! God almighty, if he talks at all now it'll be in Spanish, for sure. Do you know Spanish, son? I don't!'

But my mind was on the mermaid, not Spanish.

103

'The door's already open,' I told her indignantly. 'You don't need a key!'

'So it is! Where are my wits, for God's sake?'

And, stumbling slightly, Auntie reached the threshold, turned with studied dignity, and waved me in.

Entering Belle Lilac from the chill of the porch I seemed almost brushed by gloom, so delicate the shadows lying everywhere with dark fox cunning. Its doors a dim design in the circuit of panelling, it was a hall made grand by emptiness, by having, apparently, no chairs or tables, or even the comfort of a vase of flowers. Two features vaguely emerged — a staircase ascending hazily, and a large mantelpiece of infinite age, its marble edge faintly glimmering over a tall unused fireplace. And, instead of carpets, dark, cringing boards — whispering, beneath my uncertain feet, in half-seen lines of polished severity.

'A bit big, ain't it, son?' Auntie Alex said, standing very still beside me, her renewed clasp on my shoulder a trifle tighter. 'It's all like that. Big.'

I was silent, Auntie's words barely heard. In the centre of the mantelpiece, exquisite as ever in black and white — the tiny china mermaid!

No matter, in that halcyon moment, that behind her, like a torn flapping poster on some old Spanish wall, was the handsome face of General Franco. Ripped from Uncle Conway's magazine — the one I'd put through the door — there it hung, looking out across the hall with what — to Auntie Alex — must have been agreeable, husbandly authority. But who cared about Spanish generals? Certainly not I. Not with the mermaid to gaze at. Chill ran along my shoulder as Auntie's hand fell away. Tongue motionless, breath held in my throat, forward I crept. Then, palpitating, I was under the mantelpiece. The gritty rink of hearth beneath me, the grate bars swinging out to freeze my socks. Disregarding the vast mouldering fireplace that seemed to exude, frighteningly, odours and rustles, up I looked. There she was, all the way from Mr Edgar's house! Now I could really see her tiny smiling eyes, the pretty neck under the curls, the red, brightly modern mouth.

'Cute, ain't it, son? Though what my little man wants with a piece of blessed crock I still can't think. You'll have to put salt on her tail. See if that'll start her up!'

I should have been heedful of Auntie's breath, painfully

labouring just behind me. I should have been heedful of her arm
— cuttingly sleek as it brushed my ear — lifting to seize the
mermaid and bring it down. But I wasn't. Up, stretching, had
gone my arm too, our hands collided, and hers — clumsily
retreating, hit the mermaid. Over it toppled, to smash and
fragment in the hearth below.

What I thought I can't remember. Did I think anything? Or
was my mind, in that terrible ensuing minute as broken, useless,
as the little ornament. I may have knelt, picking up an arm,
touching a painted little hand. I remember staring into the stark
crumbly deeps of the fireplace, hearing my heart as desperate, and
as thudding, as a walled-up prisoner. Oh my mermaid! *My little
Betty*! Was that how my heart beat? Over and over. Pounding
away. Did I even believe what had happened? Everything else
was the same! The mysterious doors, the shadows throughout the
hall, the dark concertina of staircase away in the distance, the
mottled mantelpiece, the picture of General Franco, more than
ever like a tattered poster as it clung in safety to the wall.

Why did I say it? Why? Again, I don't know for sure. I just did,
that's all. And maybe it would have made no difference if I hadn't,
if I'd just stayed silent. But I said it all the same. Cut like ice from
my subconscious (had the rustlings from the fireplace been the
seed?) vicious, tearing:

'There's a mouse in the grate,' I cried, voice shrill, spiked with
passion. 'A big, white, pink-eyed mouse. In the grate!'

And I turned and looked at Auntie Alex. Her eyes were riveted,
swelling, her mouth open in a funny stretched way. The rouge on
her cheeks seemed to stand out as never before, large grotesque
islands peculiarly isolated from the flesh of nose and brow. The
black beauty spot, still there and looking now like a piece flown
upwards from the mermaid's tail, was another strange island, a
tiny, slowly turning one as Auntie's whole head, the curly hair
turning with it, seemed to revolve — her whole body, overturning,
accompanying the head in that queer, incredible slow motion.
And her expression — whatever it had been, startled, upset —
that expression, as she fell, fixed as if forever. Down, down, mouth
dark as the grate, licked only by a single helpless flare of red
tongue, that was Auntie Alex, and long before she'd struck the
floor I wanted to cry out, to tell her that I'd lied, that there wasn't
any big, white, pink-eyed mouse. And that even if there had been
I'd have scared it off!

She lay on the floor, face upwards, pink slippers pointing at the pallid ceiling. She was breathing, but in a new way, hoarse and dragged. And that funny mouth —

'Auntie Alex,' I said. 'Auntie Alex ... '

She didn't answer. Her bosom, tight against the silvery dress — like two oranges plucked from the pattern of the dress, only magnified and drained of colour — threatened to escape, to burst out and roll away, the white-peel skin aloof and mocking in the gloom.

'Aren't they the best, little man?' I could almost hear her saying. 'The most handsome tit hills, the best fruit, in all the world!'

And I'd have gladly answered, if she'd spoken, 'In the universe, Auntie Alex. In the universe!'

Trembling all over, pinioned by shock, there I stood while moments passed — helpless beside the big dark fireplace with the marble mantelpiece and ruined mermaid, and that strange recumbent body. It wasn't until I at last looked up and away, in the direction of the stairs, that I finally saw it. Lying grandly and watchfully against the curve of the skirting board — in its own way a garish, appropriate link with the limp doll that Auntie had suddenly become — was the house — formerly dwelling in the bar of the York Arms — that Uncle Conway had bought and altered and painted, the house he called his Spanish house — the large toy house he had named Madrid!

18

Feverish each hour of that black, never-ending night. Often I would wake sure that I was back in Belle Lilac, the hall shades fast around me, Auntie's body a still, flaccid obscenity on the floor. At other times I was equally sure that it was all a dream, that I'd never been inside Belle Lilac, that Auntie Alex was safely in her bed, and even the mermaid back where it belonged, in the little front bedroom of Mr Edgar's house. But then I remembered walking past, looking up at that window to see the mermaid gone. Gone where? Ah, so it wasn't a dream, the broken mermaid in the hearth, the dark pleats of ascending stairs, the doll's house against the skirting board! Yet still confusion grew: *was* it only a dream that I was in Belle Lilac stooping over Auntie Alex — only not alone with her! A rustle by the stairs, two coughs of genteel terror, and the faces of Miss Young and Miss Cuthbert peering at us, their faces like the faces of our senior clocks, excessively pale, a little yellow perhaps, with little dibs and dabs of darker markings, eyes, mouths, dark upper lips — figurings that told the time! 'Oh my gracious, look! A dreadful painted woman lying on our clean hall floor! With that dreadful child bending over her. And that open corsage! Why, dear Wells would have a fit!' 'Has she fainted? What shall we do?' 'Well, one thing we certainly cannot do is give her air. That neckline ... ' 'Oh, look. In the hearth. A shattered figurine. Of a naked girl ...' 'No, Cuthbert dear, a mermaid.' 'Very well, a mermaid then. Just as disgraceful, surely?' 'I think we'll get a bunny. One of our best angoras. It will bring her round, revive her splendidly. Hopping and snuffling over her. Rubbing its warm delicious fur all over that cold face and neck.' 'Oh please don't. One of our exquisite bunnies all covered in scent and powder and lipstick! Let the boy bring her round. He put her down there.' 'You are right, my dear. The boy put her there, the boy put her there ... '

Dreams! some dreamt that fevered night, some dreamt later, down the years, and how now to know which dreamt when? Dreams of the Spanish house against the skirting board, the windows suddenly full of mice, their twitching pink noses bursting between the shutters, sending the balcony crashing, driving General Franco and his white horse headlong through the door! And then all the squeaking triumphant mice congealing into one furry giant mass, a rabbit that grew and grew until there it was instead of the house, baring its teeth, skipping higher and higher for my throat and never quite reaching it as I fell everlastingly backwards. And the dream with Betty, the hearth full of water and Betty swimming round and round it, her pale arms rising and falling. And when I reached yearningly out, only white, hard, nasty crock — flinty flying pieces that struck towards my eyes! And the dream of Miss Cuthbert and Miss Young staggering through the hall towards the night-cloaked porch, bearing between them the weight of a huge ebony fish-tail. 'We must rid ourselves of it, Cuthbert dear. It's frightful, horrid. Then we must return and sweep up the china tit hills — isn't that what they're called? — and dispose of them too. Otherwise what would Wells think? She's like our bunnies, such an aristocrat. Oh dear, oh dear. I am positive that if they knew, our angoras would die of shock!' 'And what about the common woman? Should we not carry her out also? Though I am quite dreadfully breathless. Could we put her in the little house and close the door?' 'Oh no, we couldn't, dear. Not that. Not leave her alone with a man. A soldier. He might get off his horse ... ' 'Oh indeed, indeed. That would never, never do ... ' But she might like it, I said, in the dream. She might like it if he got off his horse and kissed her and caressed her — as I had wanted to caress the mermaid! And their swivel-eyed faces, bloodless with horror — Oh I never wanted to dream of Miss Young and Miss Cuthbert ever again!

But weren't the waking moments, especially the rare, clear-headed ones, even worse than the moments snatched in nightmare sleep? The boomerang thoughts, the perpetually returning dread. Had I really left Auntie Alex lying on the floor? Was she dead? No, no! How could Auntie Alex die? Surely, by now, she had risen and made herself a cup of tea, got a shovel and pan, cleared the hearth and gone to bed. That was what Aunt Wells would do. But suppose she hadn't? Suppose she was still there, breathing harshly, the toes of her pink slippers jutting perkily at the ceiling? Should I have told someone? But that would have meant explaining. Not just about being out of bounds, but everything! Of monstrous significance the mermaid in the hearth seemed now. What would Aunt Wells say if she knew of my obsession? She would know all. See Betty. The Betty of the kitchen. Bending over the water — a mermaid without a tail! No, the mermaid was secret. I'd wanted it more than anything in my life. In the instant of reaching for it, my nails a mere inch from the small cold curves, I'd known just how much. Serve rotten old Auntie right if she had tumbled! Smashing it like that! Wantonly, stupidly. Wicked, wicked Auntie Alex. Oh, I hated her again, hated her all the more as night pressed blackly. Why had she fallen and frightened me? She couldn't have fallen just because I'd yelled about a mouse? A rotten mouse that wasn't even there! She'd just fainted. In books — the books that Aunt Wells liked — ladies often fainted. She'd now woken up and was in bed. Or sitting on her commode. If I went back the hall would be deserted, the little Spanish house completely lost in shadow, the china bits long gathered up —

So went the black fickle night, turning gradually to a near dawn grey that was every bit as comfortless.

At breakfast Aunt Wells — surprisingly, perhaps, back in good humour, displaying a hunger as amiable as her smile — extracted with quick, deft strokes the helpless, squelching interior of a lightly boiled egg, exuding as she did so a contentment rarely seen that spring. 'This afternoon,' she told us, with a cheerful air of mystery, 'I shall be visiting Mr Mattey at his shop by the river.'

'What for, in heaven's name?' groaned Uncle Conway, clutching his head at the other end of the table. 'Not changed your mind, have you? Not buying a gun after all?'

'That egg,' Aunt Wells said, obviously full not only of egg but also Christian charity, 'was delicious. It must have been the brown shell.'

Grimacing, Uncle gulped a brimming cup of tea. 'Oh my head. This ain't the morning for eggs. Not for me!'

'Can I leave my egg, too, Aunt Wells?' I asked. 'It's got a horrid white shell. And I'm not hungry!'

'No, Gordon, you certainly cannot. Nor do I like the look of you this morning. Not a vestige of colour and your eyes dreadfully pinched. No school for you today! I shall write a note excusing you. No point in your going to school and then having a bilious attack.'

'That's why I didn't want the egg,' I gabbled. 'It's making me feel sick, Aunt Wells. It *must* be the white shell.'

Suddenly launching a characteristic outburst, 'Save your shells, my hearties!' Uncle bellowed, thumping his teaspoon, crusted morning eyelashes batting jovially. 'White or brown, save them! Wrap them in cotton wool! Pack them off to Spain. In crates marked Urgent. Shells for guns! Shells for Franco. To blast the Spanish Reds!' Adding, as he collapsed back into the chair, shooting pudgy hands to ears, 'Oh my head! This ain't the morning for shouting odds.'

'Indeed not,' said Aunt Wells thinly. 'Nor is any morning appropriate for racketing like a parade ground sergeant.'

'Hell to the Spanish Reds anyway,' Uncle croaked. 'May they be sent scampering like mice from Madrid!'

109

Vulnerability, fear. Was that what brought me, quivering, defiant, to my feet? The word mice spinning greyly in my brain? Or was my reaction solely political, a wearing of red Republican socks? Whatever the reason it came in a blink, a quick single flicker of my own crusted morning eyelashes. And, in the awakening, all tiredness fled. In that moment, the crimson curdled dust of Spain sang in my blood, the white Spanish houses shone behind my eyelids, blue gunsmoke curled. And I took my gun and joined the ranks, stood behind the sandbags, and aimed my gun. To save Madrid —

'Up the Reds!' I yelled, dominating, on tiptoe, that aghast breakfast table. 'Up up the Reds!' And my fists banged on the cloth, so that the white eggshell jumped in spiky alarm in its pale blue cup, and my cup of tea quivered and slopped.

'Death to Fatty Franco! Up up the Reds!'

Too flabbergasted to be truly angry, suddenly clasping his small round belly as if it were a fragile glass globe that had been cracked, 'You're right, Wells,' Uncle growled. 'By all means keep him at home. Boy's turning into a mad Russian Bolshevik before our very eyes. I blame that schoolteacher of his, that Mr Flood. Execrable, the things they learn these days at school. And have you noticed Sam's new watch? God knows where he got it from but he's always consulting it. Kept pulling it out all last week. Works to the minute these days, the crafty old fool. God, that's the one thing should never have been given to the lower orders. Time! The most precious thing in life, and any Jack can wear it on his wrist or put it in his pocket. Damn and blast! Watches should be chained, made inaccessible. Like they used to chain the Bible!'

'You once gave Sam an old watch and chain, Uncle Conway,' I said. 'Only he didn't like it. He said it kept running ten minutes slow.'

Uncle Conway, scowling and holding his head, didn't answer. And Aunt Wells, thinking perhaps of that afternoon, and her impending trip out, rather surprisingly gave my hair only a tender tiny tug. 'We are all slow sometimes, Gordon. Time ticks in all of us. We are all clocks. Some punctual, some reprehensibly otherwise. But all clocks. Until we stop.'

Was Auntie Alex a clock that had stopped? Perhaps that question, consciously at any rate, wasn't even present in my head.

110

Oh it had been, in the night, but in the day, the brilliantly sunlit, chilly May day ... unthinkable. Yet, as soon as Aunt Wells had departed after lunch, clad in her new spring coat and her jubilantly brave white hat, and still exuding that beatific air, off I went, out and along the pavement to Belle Lilac. Just casually, sauntering along, hands in pockets, lips puckered in a silent whistle. It was good not to be at school and — if I saw Auntie Alex — I might offer to dig her garden again. That, surely, would please her? Anyway, it would do no harm, just to take a casual glance over the Belle Lilac fence to see if Auntie was about, padding across the soil in her opulent slippers, or trudging up the path, cigarette in mouth, beauty spot frowning on her brow, to look over the gate. Ah, the gate! For when I reached the gate ... a shock! Such a shock that out from my pockets sprang my hands, and that feeble semblance of a whistle died from my lips. For the gate wasn't as it usually was, shabby and creaking as it bore the name Belle Lilac to and fro on the breeze. It was ajar all right, and creaking, but also newly lodged by a large stone. It was easy to see why. Most of the rough old wood, originally unpainted, was now streaked with white, while, over the faded blue of the old name, in all the freshness of crude black lettering — ominous as smoke in a white, bomb shattered Spanish street — a new name had been painted on. A name, a word, I already knew.

Madrid!

19

Uncle Conway, Aunt Wells and I were in a room off the hall when Mrs H — who was staying late to bake one of her Hampton specials — cake with the fruit all sunk to the bottom — came bustling in to announce, with bafflement and disapproval, that we had a caller. 'A sergeant. In uniform! Says his name is Rushing or Ruskin, I'm sure I don't know which.'

Aunt Wells, not long returned from her afternoon visit to Mr Mattey, had just called Uncle from his study and me from behind the settee where, with an old wooden tomahawk, I had been hunting for silver fish. 'We'll have a wagon of tea in here. And I'll tell you my news. Though I do not expect you, Conway, to be enraptured with it.'

'What have you and that damn Hall Mattey been up to now?' Uncle had rumbled bellicosely. 'Crawling together in the mud of Jerusalem? Kissing the hem? Washing the feet? Combing the divine hair? Whatever it is, I just feel sick.'

The pleasant pink in Aunt's cheeks deepened.

'Conway, you try my patience. Mock me if you must, but please respect a good man. Mr Mattey may, at times, seem over-zealous in his faith, but at least his eyes are on the stars.'

'The stars! The stars!' rasped Uncle Conway. 'Is that where he's going when he shuffles off? Booked his seat up there, has he? Going to die and be seated on a silvery commode and twinkle and fart and look at his big silver pocket watch all eternity long? Heaven's elder statesman? The grey old fool! I just hope I never get there. God and Hall Mattey together, breathing all over me. Ugh! Enough to kill a man. Hall Mattey! All that stuff — which, thank God, I've not had to endure — about the Saviour and the Blood of the Lamb. I'll give him lamb's blood. Inside his collar and all the way down to his miserable, shrunken buttocks! As for his Biblical miracles — I'd like to see that old car of his running on lamb's blood instead of petrol — that'd be the test!' Angrily, Uncle caught my eye. 'Gordon, why are you staring at me like that? Why aren't you at school, damn it?'

'I'm ill, Uncle Conway. Had you forgotten? Besides, it's time now for me to be home again.'

Ignoring this, 'What was he up to before electricity lit the road to Damascus for him, that's what I want to know?' Uncle rumbled on. 'Begetting, I suppose. Begetting illegitimates as fast as daisies on a lawn.'

'It seems,' Aunt said, trembling, 'that you, and that woman at Belle Lilac, still have much in common. The same unedifying flair for vulgarity. Not to mention, in your case, blasphemy. Or do you think that the way to win back her admiration? Is that what she admires? Spanish generals and blasphemy? A pretty mixture.'

They had forgotten me. I stood by the settee, silver-painted tomahawk in hand, watching them. Watching Uncle's rage, his pudgy thumb bursting round and round inside his flashing wing collar, the swelling and floundering of his tight, blue-veined waistcoat. The full hot fury of his eyes. And Aunt Wells, tall and tempestuous, freckles glaring. White cuffs rising angrily up, engulfing graceful hands. And none of us aware of the front door summons — until, that is, Mrs Hampton's flustered entrance.

'A sergeant?' Uncle Conway muttered, turning as clammily calm as his gleaming waxed eyebrows. 'God alive, what's the army want with us?'

'No, a *police* sergeant,' Mrs Hampton breathed. 'A bobby.'

'Then please show him in,' said Aunt Wells quickly, but there wasn't really need for he was already in the hall outside, left there by the affronted Mrs Hampton almost as if he were one of Sam's wheelbarrows, incontestably out of place inside a house. But the barrow was human if stiffly moving. Gloves and helmet cradled against a large flat stomach he heaved across our threshold, cropped sandy head bent in courtly bow, big sandy moustache — like convoluted Van Gogh shrubbery — writhing and flourishing outwards.

'Rushkin, Orchard Row Station. Sorry to trouble you, sir, madam.'

'Sit down, sergeant. You must take a cup of tea with us,' and, masking her concern, Aunt Wells waved the policeman to one of the large, cushion-suffocated chairs.

'Very pleasant of you, madam, but no. Too much work waiting. As a matter of fact, I wanted a word with your husband.'

'A word with me?' said Uncle Conway, startled.

'Perhaps ... ' And Sergeant Rushkin looked at Aunt Wells who, suddenly white as a swan, turned at once towards the door.

'Damnation, am I wanted for murder? There's nothing, surely, my wife can't hear?'

'Just making a few enquiries to clarify a certain matter, sir. That's all.'

Sergeant Rushkin, sitting on the edge of his chair, chunky knees upthrust, looked inside his helmet.

'It's about one of your neighbours, a Mrs Hallet. She was found, late last night, on the floor of her hall in a critical condition. Seems she lives there alone — apart, as you probably know, from a bit of regular daily help — and might not have been found if her son-in-law, a Mr Edgar, hadn't called late in the evening to check on her. Seems he promised his wife — who was down in Bristol — that he'd keep an eye on his mother-in-law.'

'Oh gracious,' Aunt Wells gasped, holding her throat. 'Mrs Hallet ill!'

'Afraid so, madam,' Sergeant Rushkin said, comfortably upturning his helmet and smoothing it over with a giant hand. 'Some sort of fit. Stroke probably. And that's why I'm making these few enquiries. You see, she was found with the front door partly open. A circumstance like that naturally calls for an enquiry or two. Not only that, but —' And he looked at Uncle Conway.

Uncle Conway glared back. 'What have I to do with it? I know nothing about the woman's collapse. Nothing at all.'

'No, sir?' The helmet, reversed, became a cup again. A cup into which the sergeant gazed, gravely and ponderingly. 'On the other hand, sir, you were seen, during the evening, painting the lady's garden gate. Most unusual, if I may say so, to be painting at night — even if it wasn't too dark. That's why you were noticed, it being relatively late and cold and the gate not your own ... Also, sir, you seemed unsteady, or so it was observed ... ' The sergeant paused, helpfully. 'However, that's not my concern. I just want to know how Mrs Hallet was, how she seemed when you saw her. Anything you can tell me, sir.'

'I didn't *see* her.' Uncle, crushed and red, seemed to be not looking at Aunt Wells rather than looking at the sergeant. 'I — I just went along and painted her gate. It — it was to be a surprise.'

'A surprise, sir? You mean, she didn't know? She didn't *know* that you were painting her gate?'

'No,' Uncle mumbled, unhappily, 'she didn't. We — we're old friends. Thought I'd surprise her, give that shabby gate of hers a brightening up. All right, maybe I shouldn't have. Maybe I should have asked her permission first. But I didn't. Put it down, if you like, to my having visited the pub. No law against that, is there? A man having a few drinks, and then trying to do an old friend a good turn?'

'I see, sir,' Sergeant Rushkin said, sounding, now, no happier than Uncle. 'Then did you happen to perceive that the front door was open? Did you see or hear any one or anything — including Mrs Hallet — during the time that you were painting the gate?'

'No I didn't, sergeant. Never even glanced towards the house.

And, at that distance, probably wouldn't have noticed that the door was ajar. Unless the lights were on.'

'Quite, sir. Then there's no information at all that you can help me with?'

'Damn it, no. Woman must have opened the door herself before she collapsed. Ain't that feasible?'

'She was found some way from the door, sir. However — '

Shrugging beefily, Sergeant Rushkin rose at last. 'Well, apologies for troubling you both — '

Aunt Wells, who had been standing rigidly, rustled into sudden, perfunctory movement.

'Thank you for calling, sergeant. It's terrible news. Poor Betty — Mrs Hallet's daughter. She, of course — '

'Has naturally been informed. And now, madam, if you don't mind — '

As Sergeant Rushkin stepped on quiet, giant feet to the door I must have moved, for he stopped, looking curiously around.

'Hardly noticed you, young fellow,' he said companionably. 'What's that you've got? An axe?'

'A tomahawk,' I contradicted, flushing. 'For killing silver fish. They're everywhere. Aunt Wells says so.'

'Well,' said Sergeant Rushkin, grinning, white gloves tapping cheerfully on the helmet's rim, 'so long as you don't scalp policemen with it. Eh, madam?'

20

After showing the sergeant out Aunt Wells turned and went to the stairs, walking quickly and erectly up them without a glance towards the room where, probably, Uncle Conway stood recovering. Since Aunt Wells had left the closing of the front door to me I stood a moment watching Sergeant Rushkin moving with dark blue dignity under the trees, noting, too, the sudden appearance of Sam from behind one of them, skywards thrusting rump excitedly clasped by an earthy hand as he, also, watched the officer's departure. 'I was proper a-staggered, Mister Gordon,' he said later, scratching inside the hairiest of his nostrils. 'What's Mister Big been up to then?'

When I shut the front door the hall, despite its crammed condition, seemed chillingly to expand. Even the Grecian lady with the urn on her head had never looked colder. I heard Uncle coughing — short restless coughs — I heard the squeak of his shoes as he paced the carpet, and I smelt the aroma of a freshly lit Craven A. Moving to the foot of the stairs I stared upwards. At last, half-heartedly, not quite knowing where to go or what to do, I too ascended. At the top, on the musty landing, I paused to listen. There was a sound, no more than a rustle. When I peered inside one of the bedrooms I saw Aunt sitting in a chair by the window. Sitting tautly, looking out at the garden, though whether she really saw the garden I do not know. Across her lap she had placed a silken, pale green jacket, as if, perhaps, she needed something, even cool silk, to cover and warm her motionless, white-cuffed hands. She wasn't crying, the rustle may have been no more than the jacket pulled from the bed, or a tiny shift of her feet on the carpet, or even a sigh.

If I, too, made a rustle, standing in the doorway, Aunt Wells didn't hear. Quietly I turned, flitting away along the passage. Until I heard Uncle Conway on the stairs, his breathing, as the short legs mounted, increasingly puffy and distraught. I turned, creeping almost fearfully back, wondering what he might have to say to Aunt Wells, and what Aunt Wells might have to say to him.

At first, nothing. Only Uncle's heavy breathing. Looking through the half open door I saw him a little way inside, hands clasped together below rear jacket rim, fingers squirming. And the fingers, wriggling hotly on, seemed to mark the seconds, a white clock face turned maggoty and alive as it clung to Uncle's seat.

'I never told you, did I, Conway, why I went to Mr Mattey's shop today?' And, briefly, Aunt Wells turned her head.

'Tell me, then,' said Uncle, swelling defiantly. 'If you must —'

'Last night, after the service, I was approached — asked if I would care to become one of the trustees of the mission. In place of Mr Frigatoon-Bewdley, an old gentleman who died recently. Considering the short time that I've known them all, I was astounded. And delighted. Not, of course, that you would

116

appreciate my feelings, Conway. Delight, for you, is obviously the ceaseless absorption of wines and spirits. Not the offer, and acceptance, of responsibility.'

Moving suddenly away, so that the doorway filled with light, 'The old story,' I heard Uncle mutter. 'They're after our money. Damn Reds, all of them!'

'This afternoon,' Aunt continued, evenly, 'I went and told Mr Mattey of my acceptance. I said that I'd be delighted to be a trustee. And that I would discharge that duty to the best of my endeavour.'

'All right, woman. So? You're mad, but if that's what you wish — '

'Don't you see, Conway? *Can't* you see?' Aunt Wells, the pale green jacket unruffled across her lap, her face, in cold profile, turned to the colder window glass, still looked calm. Only her voice betrayed change, its tone suddenly jagged, fretful. 'Am I being fair, that is the question you make me ask. Am I being fair in becoming a trustee when — Oh Conway, isn't it obvious? Can't you honestly see? Aren't you aware of what you're *doing?*'

Uncle suddenly pacing the bedroom out of my sight, his perturbed striding making of the door crack a dark, snatching flicker.

'All right, Wells. I was drunk! Had had one or two before I'd even been to the pub. And then, at the pub, a few more. But, damn it, when you're ... '

'In your cups? To use one of poor Mrs Hallet's pet phrases.'

'Yes,' Uncle mumbled. 'Exactly. In cups. In fact, damn it, don't remember doing anything at all, let alone painting gates. If it hadn't been for that blasted sergeant saying people saw me, and a smear of paint on yesterday's suit — which I saw only this morning — I'd have denied the whole blasted thing. But, if I did do it, so what? No more, in essence, than a friendly act. A kindness even. The sort of daft caper your Christianity preaches. Paint thy neighbour's gate and thou shalt be blessed above even the kings of the earth, or some such tommy rot! So why the blasted fuss? I only painted the woman's gate. Hall Mattey would give me a medal for it. It's not adultery. Not like painting the town red inside her bed!'

Suddenly not even the squeak of Uncle's shoes. Aunt very still. Head, hands under the jacket, all still.

'So I've got to be window-dressing, have I? For the sake of your Bolshevik, hymn howling friends! A good pious lily-white little Jehovahian! And teetotal to boot. Cabbage, Wells, cabbage! I'll drink my drink and say my piece and damn the world! Not that it needs damning. It's damned already.'

An hour later Aunt Wells wasn't in the house. Uncle Conway, taken by surprise, poked irately among the garments on the old hall stand. One of the warmer winter coats, perhaps in deference to a chilly evening, was absent from its hook. And the tall plum coloured hat, the oldest of Aunt's hats — never stored in a box, always on the stand as a good quick plain choice for the emergencies of everyday — was also absent from its peg. Wherever Aunt was going, she wasn't surely going to visit anyone?

'Never told me she was going out,' Uncle Conway grumbled. 'Where the devil's she gone to now?'

'I think she's gone to sit on the platform of the railway station, Uncle Conway,' I said.

It had been, to say the least, immensely strange, the manner in which — on one of our shopping expeditions during the early part of that spring, and at a time shortly after discovering the identity of her new neighbour — Aunt Wells had stopped in the centre of the small humped bridge over the railway lines. As though fingers had tugged at her stiffly hanging elbow — she bore a fully loaded basket — plucking her to the parapet, inviting her to view. Yet, at that moment, there was nothing to see. Only the quiet Saturday morning imprisoned in the pleasant, scrubby, high banked cutting below. But Aunt's immobility was no idle whim, nor was she hoping and waiting for a passing train. She was looking down at the station a little way along from the bridge. On her face such brooding, such a wistfulness. Then, as though struggling with herself, with a suddenly awakened temptation (had the devil shown her a kingdom and invited her to take it?), and for once not struggling too hard, she made a startling suggestion. It was — though I didn't know it at the time — the start of a practice, of a refuge that Aunt was to indulge whenever, that harrowing spring, we passed the station. A harmless enough refuge — rooted in nostalgia — which only Aunt herself, with her deep and unvarying loyalty, could have questioned. The faintest of furrows on her brow, she made her surprising, almost shy suggestion.

118

'Gordon, just for a short while, we'll rest.'

'Rest, Aunt Wells? On the bridge?'

'No, Gordon. In the railway station. Though we are not, let me emphasize, catching a train.'

Off she went, quickly, down the short white ancillary road sweeping to the serrated roof and sunlit brick of the station entrance. Trudging after her into the station, I began to feel excited. And puzzled. Suddenly she was as apart, as absorbed, as when locked into that small book of love poems.

'Morning, luv,' said a porter on the platform, pushing a trolley just to the east of her new spring coat.

Had Aunt even heard him? She sat down on a bench, tiredly shut her eyes. Of what was she thinking?

'This station, Gordon,' Aunt said presently, without opening her eyes. 'The platform opposite. Where ... where we —'

And her voice held a break, a tiny stumbling of sorrow. Her gloved fingers gripped each elbow painfully deep.

Impulsively, a little scared, I put my hand on her arm.

'What is it, Aunt Wells? What's the matter?'

And then, moved by my own brash instinct, 'It's your beloved, isn't it, Aunt Wells? That's who you're thinking of?'

Her beloved (to use Uncle Conway's mocking phrase) here, in this station! And, full of wonder, I looked at the platform opposite.

'He *was* here, wasn't he, Aunt Wells? This is where he went off to the Great War?'

How clever I was. All soldiers caught trains to go off to war.

Aunt Wells said quietly, 'Yes, Gordon, he was here. The young man I once hoped to marry. Yes, he was leaving for the war. He came across the lines, carrying his baggage on his shoulder. He was late. There was scarcely time for us to talk.'

I fidgeted, disappointed.

'What happened, Aunt Wells? Before he crossed the lines did he get a bar of chocolate out of that Nestlé's machine? Was there time for that?'

'I don't remember if there were chocolate machines then, Gordon. And, really, nothing happened. The train came in. We kissed goodbye. And that was that. I never saw him again. Ypres —'

And Aunt looked across the lines, as if recalling, in minutest

119

detail, that scene of farewell. Or was she only looking at the dingy waiting-room directly opposite, at its tawdry brown seating, grimy walls —

They shall grow not old, as station waiting-rooms grow old —

Out of nowhere, and after a long silence — and why I said it goodness knows! 'Aunt,' I said. 'Do you love Uncle Conway? Even though he wasn't killed in the war?'

She looked startled, and then, suddenly, she looked shiningly clean. As if, unwittingly, I'd dusted her mind, restored — at any rate for a little while — its bright perspective.

'Yes, Gordon, of course I do. Of course I love your Uncle Conway.'

21

What, as she lay in the town infirmary, did Auntie Alex think about? Did she think at all? What was her condition? Could she speak? Was she recovering? Or was she simply suspended, not moving one way or the other, besieged and merely surviving — victory or surrender in balance — rather like Madrid? For this was not the spring of Madrid's fall — that lay ahead, many months ahead. Still to be uttered La Pasionaria's speech honouring the International Brigades as, the course of the Civil War closing against the Republican cause like an oyster, they departed from Spain: 'We shall not forget you, and when the olive tree of peace puts forth its leaves again, mingled with the laurels of the Spanish Republic's victory — come back!' Still in the future the propaganda flights of Franco's planes: loaves of bread, manna dropped to the starving capital's streets (Republican planes dropped shirts and socks). Poor Madrilenos, fated to live on lentils and bread, only the constant siege to stiffen their will and muscle. The final agony, then, yet to be. As for Auntie Alex — were not the days of her illness equal to Madrid's years of travail? Auntie Alex, so much younger than the old Spanish city —

though, at times, just as hot, as passionate and wilful! And as isolated, as lonely?

During that long precarious week following Auntie's seizure I too, knew isolation. I remember constantly patrolling, moving constantly from clock to clock. Checking, making sure that each one ticked. Afraid, each day, that somewhere, somehow, a clock would be silent — its hands black streaks of death on pallid papery skin. For once, long ago, a clock had stopped! The despondent old grandfather clock in the dark, Egyptian mummy-tall casing, lord — along with an old Aspidistra on a table — of a particularly sepulchral corner. Suddenly dead as a doornail, its pendulum still, its ticking lost in dusty silence! According to Uncle Conway a tiny, almost invisible mouse had got inside and stopped the works!

The shop was just off the square. In each of the two top corners of its window skipped creamy woolly toy lambs. Over the window, in fancy, limpid blue lettering: The Baby Shop: Your Cherub's Paradise.

I hadn't looked at the shop until today, and certainly wouldn't have but for seeing, directly in front of it, insecurely lodged against the kerb, an old bicycle, and, on the pavement, peering earnestly through the window at the delights within, Mr Edgar. Mr Edgar in his usual dark baggy suit and startling white collar, the hard dark hat sitting with difficulty on his head as its brim butted the glass. Adjusting my satchel — I was on my way home from Tuesday afternoon school — I crept across the tree lined road and up behind the unsuspecting little man. He didn't turn — even when I cleared my throat in a nasty, tigerish growl. Wondering what so absorbed him I, too, gazed into the window. What a shock! Never, in all my life, had I seen such an assembly of rubbish. In the centre of both the window and a playpen was a pram, black and gleaming. Next to it an idiotic high baby chair of light oak with a blue seat. Under the chair a bead frame, the beads in tiny, irregular, bombastically coloured groupings. There was a cot, made up as if ready for some gurgling infant. Rattles! Baby clothes, little dresses. And, scattered about the floor of the window among the rattles, dummies for sucking on! Ugh! If on my own I would have turned in instant flight. But there stood Mr Edgar, right beside me, the corners of his mouth puckered in wistful contemplation, adrift in some incomprehensible, all engul-

121

fing day dream. What on earth was he looking at? Surely not a tiny enamel chamber pot intended for some squeaking baby's pink and white behind? The pram then?

'You sissy, Mr Edgar,' I said, and then, firmly, recalling Mrs Hampton's favourite word of the moment, the way everything was somehow positive, a positive disgrace or a positive nuisance or a positive liberty, 'I think that you're a positive sissy!'

Mr Edgar turned, deep eyes shining, rubbing pale knuckles against his pear shaped nose. From his mild expression I knew he'd not heard me.

'Ah,' he said, after a moment. 'My young man, isn't it? Young Gordon. How are you, lad?'

'It's all sissy,' I muttered. 'That stuff there. In the shop.'

Mr Edgar looked amazed. And suddenly slightly embarrassed — as if caught out in some hugely personal indulgence. Scraping his fingers around the inside of his high, shoe box white collar, 'You're mistaken, lad,' he said. 'There is nothing — sissy, did you say? — about a shop catering for babies and toddlers. All the things that you see are useful and necessary, of that I do assure you.'

'Rattles!' I said. 'Teats! I'd rather suck bubble gum.'

'I'm sure, I'm sure.' Taking off his hat Mr Edgar mopped his brow. 'But then, lad, you're not a baby, are you?'

Irritably, aware that he was right and I wrong, aware, too, of sudden fury, not only for the shop but also towards Mr Edgar, 'Anyway,' I said, 'I think it's all damned nonsense. That's what Uncle Conway says. All cabbage and damn it.'

Turning sadly away Mr Edgar plodded gently to his bicycle. Freeing the pedal from the kerb he balanced the machine upright, giving the handlebars a slow thoughtful twist to and fro, as if to clear them from some invisible gluey restraint. His nose, I saw, was sweating. It always turned to dew when he was embarrassed, and sure enough — letting the bicycle collapse against his suit — he suddenly produced the flowing dark wine coloured folds of an outsize handkerchief — burying his nose not to blow it but just to dry the glimmering skin.

'Well, young man, I'd like to buy you a lemonade, but too busy. Expected at home. What with one thing and another — no time to be idle. Work, the house, Betty's mother at the hospital. Seriously ill — '

'You weren't too busy to look into that shop!' I muttered, not feeling quite as fierce as I sounded, a quick terrible guilt staining my cheeks. Seriously ill! Oh that mouse, why had I invented it? My thoughts lurched, back I swept, back to Belle Lilac on Sunday evening, with the strangely vulpine shadows in the hall and on the stairs, the gloomy mantelpiece with its single jewel — the blissfully lovely mermaid that looked like Betty. Then Auntie's hand on my shoulder, both of us moving forward, until, free, I was in the fireplace, reaching, reaching for the mermaid —

'But then, lad, you're not a father, are you?' Mr Edgar said. Carefully, opening a worn purse (an impression of the head and slender neck of Nefertiti fading away on the leathery outside) he gave me a whole incredible glittering shilling before putting away, along with the wine coloured, exploding-like-a-rose handkerchief, the shabby purse. 'Or, like me, a father-to-be! Makes a difference, I'm sure.' And, humping amiably onto the saddle of his bike, off he pedalled under the spring trees — until out of sight.

22

Saturday, the Saturday following the fateful Sunday of Auntie Alex's collapse, arrived — for May — chillingly and stingingly. Sam grumbled about plants a-frosting in the bud, Mrs Hampton said she was again wearing her matriarchal woollen vests, and Enoch Balsom, in elegant ear muffs, called round to tell us, testily, that he did not think an ex-Birmingham Lord Mayor like Neville Chamberlain would ever make a good prime minister. On the preceding Wednesday — the day after my encounter with Mr Edgar — Aunt Wells had returned from visiting Betty to report that Mrs Hallet was still very poorly, hardly talking. Then, on Friday, a letter from Miss Young saying that in Monday evening's paper — our local paper, which she took by post — she had been shocked to read about a widow being found ill in dear Belle Lilac. What an unhappy thing. Perhaps she should never have left Belle Lilac. 'Who would have thought that it would be sold again so soon? And to a public house person! I vaguely remember, at a

Christian jumble sale, a heavily painted woman picking up some undergarment and holding it against herself in the most vulgar fashion. 'That's Mrs Hallet, from the Arms,' the curate said. Perhaps he was misinformed, as I am sure your dear husband would not paint a gate — especially a *front* gate — for such a person!' After that it took Aunt Wells — who hadn't seen the item in the paper — an hour of prayer in the library before she found the resolution not to rush off to Mr Mattey, resigning the new trusteeship. Mr Mattey, though, had his own woes. 'Charlotte no longer with us', he wrote Aunt Wells in a letter delivered that same morning. 'Ignoring her marital status, she has absconded with a married man! Someone she met when she visited the Co-op to buy raisins. A Mr Price ... who, I believe, stood for the council as Labour and Co-operative. Should have told you, and our other friends on Sunday last, but couldn't. Too ashamed. Yet the Lord is with us always. Lo, even in the depths!'

That afternoon, returning from school, I had found Aunt opening the curtains of one of the bedrooms and making the bed. Clearly it had been used that afternoon — the pillows squeezed, the air as crumpled with scent and *unfreshness* as the bed was crumpled.

'Aunt Wells,' I said, 'you and Uncle Conway haven't been to sleep?'

Aunt blushed. 'No, Gordon. Burying the hatchet.'

'Hatchet, Aunt Wells? What hatchet? You haven't buried my tomahawk?'

'A gate, Gordon. That's what I've buried.'

First a hatchet, now a gate. Was she dotty?

'If one doesn't bury certain things,' Aunt said brightly, ruffling my bewildered head, 'they go on festering. Yes, Gordon, even gates!'

Resenting this puzzling skittishness, 'Are you going to the railway station tonight, Aunt Wells?' I asked. 'Are you going to sit on the platform and think about beloved?'

Again, Aunt blushed. 'No, Gordon. Nor shall I go ever again, unless to catch a train. Time wasted is time lost. Time lost is love lost. One day, perhaps, you'll understand.'

That evening we saw that Auntie Alex's number in the local paper, her Infirmary number, listing her among the very poorlies, had been moved to 'poorly'. And, on Saturday, her number wasn't in at all.

124

'I'm sure that's a good sign,' Aunt Wells said. 'I saw Betty this afternoon in town — her mother's speech is much improved. I'm so glad. Although the poor girl only hinted at it, her mother's drinking greatly increased after moving to Belle Lilac — which can't have helped. All that nonsense about being in love with General Franco — about believing that her husband may have returned to life! Betty herself looked awful, very pale — apparently she's pregnant — and I invited her to take tea with me in Dapperings, but she said she was on her way to the York Arms.'

'York Arms?' Uncle growled. 'Why the devil was she going there? Not her home now, is it?'

'She said that an old empty doll's house which used to be kept in the bar had turned up at Belle Lilac, and that she didn't see it there the night before her mother's collapse. Mrs Hallet had gone round to say goodbye to Betty who was leaving for Bristol in the morning, and Betty had escorted her mother back home. Rather than pester Mrs Hallet about it at this time, she thought she'd pop and ask the landlord. Conway, what is the matter?'

'Nothing,' Uncle groaned, patting his waistcoat as if the fountain pen sticking out of one of its top pockets were a blood rimmed dagger. 'Nothing at all.'

The doorbell rang. When Aunt Wells came back she looked strangely paler.

'It's Betty, Conway. Asking if she may see you. In private!'

I didn't see Betty that Saturday. Only heard her. How well I remember that unique occasion. For Aunt Wells eavesdropped! For the first time in my life I saw her outside a closed door, hovering, eyes pinched dark freckles as she looked unseeingly along the hall. And when I joined her at the door — she didn't tell me to leave! It was as if what was being said inside the room were too important to risk the slightest wrangling or movement. Only later, hurrying me away, did she reveal her abhorrence. 'Come, Gordon. We must not be caught ignominiously listening at the door. To listen at all is unworthy, but to be caught listening is not only to feel unworthy, but also to look it!' If only she could have been as coolly indifferent as the nearby Grecian lady. No closed doors, no coxcomb-red, embarrassed, spluttering husband in *her* virtuously static life!

'Well, Betty, what's up? What's the blasted mystery?'

'I would like to know exactly *when* you took mother that doll's house. I've had a feeling all along that something happened that night to upset her.'

'All right, damn it, all right. I took it her that Sunday evening. Early — before going to the pub. She was perfectly all right when I left her, I swear it. In fact she was pleased. She'll tell you that herself. Ask her, for God's sake! We had a drink together. Like old times. Damn it, deep down I'm fond of Alex — '

Aunt Wells' breath, suddenly so fiercely drawn it seemed to fill the hall.

'Then why haven't you spoken of all this?' Betty said. 'Is it because — '

Uncle Conway also took a thunderous breath. Its scornful rasp came clearly, cuttingly, through the door. 'Of course not! Not *that* much like old times. I simply took her the redecorated house. A — a gesture to remind her of the old days at the Arms. She was tickled pink with it. Said it would come in for her grandchild. Then we drank a toast before I left. To General Franco! Nothing, damn it, for any one to be ashamed of in *that*. All the same, didn't really want my wife to know I'd called. Upset enough over my painting the gate. Why I did that can't think, except it must have seemed a good idea at the time. Ah the grape, Betty, the grape. It's the mistress, and master, of us all!'

23

Sunday, having finally arrived, was colder than even Saturday had been. Gloomy too — at least inside our house. Doors opened and closed at random as people hurriedly shut themselves away from one another. When — prowling around wondering why Aunt hadn't gone to church — I knocked over the dustbin lid and saw the little volume of love poems that Auntie Alex had given Aunt Wells, I took it out, rubbed off the ash, and put it in my pocket. Why had Aunt discarded it, I wondered? And why was she crying so much, or at any rate drooping around with that wet, uncomfortable look? All Uncle had done was spruce up that silly old doll's house and take it to Mrs Hallet who — Uncle said — had liked it. Of course he should have told Sergeant Rushkin, but so, perhaps, should I! Not about the house, but about the mouse! What if Betty were to discover about that? Auntie Alex might tell her. The thought had kept me awake all night. And then, with dawn rolling like a huge grey milk churn high across town square, my mind had cleared. I'd say that there *had* been a mouse! A real one. Then I couldn't be blamed. *There had been a mouse in the fireplace,* I'd seen it move, and had told Auntie Alex! Under the blankets a chilling shudder had run through me. She was getting better, and one day I was going to have to see her again. What would she say? And do? Tell Betty, in front of me, about my wicked longing for the naked mermaid? Oh how terrible that would be. *Betty would surely know that the mermaid looked like her.* And Auntie, laughing grimly, one stern thumb tapping on her beauty spot, 'My little man likes naked fish-tail ladies, don't you, son? Stroking them up till the time when you're a big big fisherman and can catch yourself a real one. Just like my Noel caught me!' Oh dear, oh yes — that's what she'd say. Why, almost better if she died —

The sharp, guilty thought struck at me again, as it had in bed. Quickly, shivering, I went indoors.

Uncle Conway was in his study, looking with loathing at the flask on his desk — as if it were a soldier at dawn, full of vigour and war at a time when decent folk shouldn't be disturbed.

'Uncle Conway,' I said, 'Where's Aunt Wells?'

'Ah, Wells,' he said. 'Blessed woman knows, that's obvious. She ain't speaking to me! Crying everywhere like a tipped kettle. Damn it, why can't a man be trusted? These days I'm pure as the driven snow. Beware, lad, of righteous ladies. Easily upset. Easily made to cry.'

'Is Auntie Alex a righteous lady, Uncle Conway? Is she pure as the driven snow?'

'Your Auntie Alex,' said Uncle, flushing, 'is as difficult to conquer these days as Madrid! Not that I'd try mind. Off with you, boy, I'm reluctantly thirsty.'

'When you say conquer, Uncle Conway, do you mean kiss? And would you have liked to kiss Mr Mattey's daughter? I know she's only a big daft cabbage, but — '

Uncle's colour deepened. Briefly his fingers flew to his collar,

127

scrabbling hotly. 'Stupid woman! Daft as the cherry on her hat. Falling in love over a pound of raisins! Co-op raisins, damn it. Going off with that blasted Socks. Seduced by that counter crawling ladler of dried currants. No, boy. I don't want to kiss her. Not only that, daughter of a preacher. Be like kissing the Bible. Only want to kiss your aunt, my boy, kiss your aunt.'

Aunt Wells, looking far from kissable in a tall twisting dust bonnet, was downstairs cleaning through the cabinet of cut glass in the dining room.

'Uncle Conway's upstairs, Aunt Wells,' I said. 'Drinking. But he says he wants to kiss you.'

'Gordon, you should have gone to church!'

'Aunt Wells,' I said, quickly, 'most houses have mice living in them, don't they?'

'Sadly, Gordon, yes. Though at the moment we seem remarkably free of them.'

'Those rabbit droppings,' I said, 'that Auntie Alex found in her house. Could — could they have been left by mice?'

Putting down a fluted glass sugar bowl Aunt turned and stared at me.

'Don't be stupid, Gordon. Anyway, I doubt there are mice there. That was just a ridiculous story told by Sam to upset... Mrs Hallet. And now, if you don't mind, I'm busy — '

'Will Auntie Alex die, Aunt Wells?'

'Only God can answer that, Gordon.'

'If we don't pray, will she die?'

'Gordon!'

In the afternoon I stayed in the garden, bundled up against the May cold, tossing a cricket ball at an old tree stump. Aunt had said that I could be excused Sunday school because of accompanying her to the mission that evening.

'Is Uncle driving us? In the car?'

'Certainly not, Gordon. I've no intention of troubling your Uncle.'

Shortly before six o'clock the noise of a vehicle was heard in the drive. The lake of Galilee dress, too light for the unseasonable weather, had been passed over for a twin set, pearls, and long tweed skirt. Over this a warm coat. Thus apparelled Aunt Wells took sail for the door. Skin as polished as the glass of the dining room cabinet, I dutifully followed. Where Uncle Conway was I didn't know, nor did Aunt. He had been glimpsed at intervals in

128

house and garden; glassily studying flowers, vanishing up the stairs with an irate unsteady twinkle of legs and rotund rear, rolling from the kitchen holding a cold pork chop, leaning intently over the Grecian lady in the hall — flask in hand — as if pondering the advisability or otherwise of filling up her urn with whisky. And, just occasionally, we had heard him. 'Where's my Spanish galleon? Where's my ship of war? Wanna fight, wanna *fight*. Yes, sir. Yes, General Franco. At your service, sir. Shoot my wife? Yes, sir! Bury her outside? Under the old olive tree? Yes, sir!'

In the porch Aunt carefully shut the door, then turned to face the drive. 'Oh,' she gasped, the unhappiness already on her brow suddenly compounded by what she saw. 'Oh dear —'

Daniel Damascus, the old, squarely built black car, was not to be seen anywhere under the trees. Instead, backed onto our drive, there stood a truck. Not a particularly clean truck, it looked — especially in the clear evening light — as if it might have been used for anything — even coal. A broken tailboard had been left hanging. Rust adorned most of the metal strips along the truck sides. The high cab looked greyly dilapidated. Ropes and a chain were visible on the gritty boards — the only other freight a squashed cigarette, and sacking the colour of old dark earth.

From the cab, exuding a kind of forced aplomb from under his rakishly angled trilby hat, dropped Mr Mattey, watch in hand, pink bow tie briefly askew as his jacket lapels pushed inwards. As he approached, striding leanly, I observed with fresh distaste his fulsome elderly eyebrows, the streaks of yellow in his large, craggy moustache, the rogue, bristly hairs on chin and long grey neck. Taking one of Aunt's hands in a brisk, untidy shake, he still found time to look at me. 'Ah, our young friend. The lad of infinite possibilities. We are to be honoured, then.' Adding, softly, 'Dear madam, you look troubled? If you are thinking of my sorrow, of what dear Charlotte has done, please, I beg you, don't. We all have sorrows. Sorrow is the cloth we wear. Until, alas, the grave.'

'The lorry,' Aunt said, after a pause. 'I was a little —'

'Taken aback? And why not? Not everyone's idea of transport, I must confess. Not half as elegant as a taxi, or a car. Indeed, if your good husband is available —'

'No,' Aunt said, quickly. 'No, I think not. But what —'

'A last minute contretemps. Daniel Damascus, alas, refuses to start. Not a sound from the old jalopy. Though capable of roaring

129

like a whole pride of lion, he now stands silent. Come. Come and meet my good friend and neighbour, Mr Greengage Yancey.'

A small sinewy man had appeared from the other side of the cab. The owner, apparently, of the beastly lorry, he stood uneasily before us twirling a purple, heavily peaked cloth cap. The blue suit, probably his best, looked damp and woolly, as if it had been freshly sponged for Sunday.

'Wiv pleasure,' he said, nodding shyly at Aunt.

'There'll just be room in the cab,' Mr Mattey said, proprietorially taking Aunt's elbow. 'And you needn't worry about your clothes. Mr Yancey has most scrupulously cleaned the inside seat. Haven't you, Greengage?'

'Wiv two dusters, one damp, one dry,' said Mr Yancey. His blue eyes seemed to water, then wade nervously about. The swallow in his throat rose and fell.

'Are your dusters old socks?' I asked, glaring. 'Aunt Wells has old socks belonging to Uncle Conway for dusting.'

'Gordon! Not for dusting, for polishing brass! Oh dear, don't children let us down? No doubt, Mr Yancey, you have one of your own. A child, I mean.'

'Five,' said Mr Yancey, gulping. 'Five nippers.'

'But good, eh, Greengage?' said Mr Mattey jocularly. 'Good, clean children. And quiet as mice.'

Mice! My heart turned over.

After a quick look behind her towards the house, Aunt Wells, with all the majesty she could summon, ascended to the cab, sliding inside and along the seat with both hands holding her coat and skirt, furling them tightly as though to minimize any contact the garments might have with surviving grime. After which she took a deep breath, and looked palely out through the window.

'Now, lad, up with you,' purred Mr Mattey, the nails of his cold fingers scratching on my neck. 'Show your strength, Samson!'

Up I went, sliding on short polished trousers to join Aunt Wells along the seat.

'And now,' said Mr Mattey merrily, hat pushed back, grey hair poking stiffly out, 'up *I* come! The righteous shall be last, but first in the kingdom, eh, little Adam?' And, to my discomfort, gripping my bare knee, Mr Mattey hauled himself in onto the squalling leather seat. Then, turning breathlessly — it was already a squash — he nodded approvingly down at the cap twisting, moist-eyed

Mr Yancey. 'This dear good friend of mine. Indispensable. This is not the first time his truck has turned up trumps in an emergency.'

Blushing, Mr Yancey slammed the door and scurried to the other side, where, after gingerly moving in beside Aunt Wells, he proceeded to dwarf himself under the large purple cap.

'Before we start,' said Mr Mattey, 'shall we pray? Not for our safety — what danger can there be on England's quiet and pleasant roads — but for the success of our evening at the mission? That country Bethel known as Welcome. That little house so dear to our Father.'

Off, hastily, to be twirled all over again, came Mr Yancey's cap. Aunt Wells tightly shut her eyes, inclining her head. I did the same — with one eye left warily open. Being crammed next to Mr Mattey, that man who so persistently mocked me, was enormously unsettling. I could smell his breath, dry as an old cask. I could feel his lanky body, hard as that silvery cherubic watch forever in and out of his chilly fingers.

'That His hand be lowered to bless us, and comfort us. Amen. That His voice be heard. Amen. That His grace endow us all with love. Amen.'

The last Amen of all came from the engine which, after rumbling quietly away, now gave vent to a grumpy jolting that whipped open Aunt's eyes and made even Mr Mattey blink. Several rattling moments later and the truck began to move, under the trees and down the drive.

It was a strange journey, that drive through the chilly sunlit May evening. Country grunts and shouts — wind howlings too — merged eerily with the spluttery grind of Mr Greengage Yancey's truck. Conversation was rare, Mr Yancey too humble to expound, Aunt, sardine compressed, feeling perhaps at a disadvantage, and Mr Mattey — due on this particular evening to preach — meditating — his lips, under the grey moustache, occasionally moving excitedly, his thickly veined hands and bony wrists occasionally fleeing the crumpled mustiness of his sleeves to dance nervily in the air above his lap. These stirrings of a fermenting pulpit passion I managed to ignore. Not so Aunt Wells.

'You are a declamatory man, Mr Mattey,' I remember her saying as we threaded a lane full of cows and a gaping farmer.

'How wonderful to command words. To use them as a wise master uses his servants. I envy you.'

'The infinitely mysterious gift of tongues, dear madam,' said Mr Mattey, gratified, wiping that grey-rock moustache. 'The infinitely mysterious gift of tongues.'

Later, turning to the driver, graciously involving that neglected man, 'You know, Mr Yancey,' Aunt said, 'I've mixed feelings about this increasing use of the motor engine. Such a pity that freight nowadays depends so much less on our noble old friend, the horse.'

Touching his cap as if thankful to be noticed, his blue eyes wading wildly, 'Wiv respect, mam,' said Mr Yancey, 'but modern roads ain't grass.' Hunched before the wheel like a purple capped gnome, he seemed suddenly to glow with profundity and ill humour. 'Ask Caesar.'

'Ah, the Romans. You mean they built real roads, splendid roads?' Aunt said.

Mr Yancey looked amazed. 'Caesar's my canine, mam. A big white canine wiv a black patch. But even he don't like modern roads. Getting busy, getting smelly. No good for horses, neither. Wiv respect.'

'Ah yes,' cried Mr Mattey, butting passionately in as though he could not bear to be left out. 'Dogs, horses, all God's creatures, all creation His! Right, dear madam? Am I not right?'

I remembered the first time that I had seen Mr Mattey, behind his counter, creeping, humped and sinister.

'Ferrets, too?' I asked, looking fearfully up. 'Does Jesus notice them, too, like the sparrows?' I paused, remembering the rifles that Mr Mattey sold. 'And does Jesus sell people guns to shoot bunnies and foxes?'

But Aunt was pinching my arm, and Mr Mattey, instead of answering with his usual incomprehensible humour, gave me a bleak look before closing his eyes — the shadow pulpit pantomime of rehearsing for his sermon starting up all over again.

Journey's end came abruptly, the truck shaking to a halt in the little twisting lane. As the engine died the strains of the harmonium came wafting through the open door of the nearby mission into the cab. Carefully and quietly, awed by the sweetly febrile sound, we descended to the lane. Aunt Wells looked shining, her breath reverently bated. Mr Yancey, his two wading blue eyes now totally drenched, took off his cap, doubled it over and, with the peak, gave the seat of his bright blue trousers a hard quick deferential rub. Even I felt a continuing awe — until I remembered that the harmonium was only being played by silly little Mr Edgar.

'God saying welcome to His people through His servant, George Edgar,' said Mr Mattey softly, as though reading my mind. 'It is as simple, and as wonderful, as that.'

'Deal out the guns, deal out the bloody guns!' croaked a voice, which, rising, changed to a bellicose biting sibilancy. 'Face to the shun! Arouse battal-onions! Conquer! Shpain, free! Shpain, arise ... arise!' And then a dreadful thumping, like pounding fists.

The four of us, rooted in the lane, gazed quickly about. I even bent, peering into the hedge.

'The guns, I shay, the guns,' droned the voice. 'deal 'em out. We're here! We've reached Mad — Madrid!'

'Goshums,' said Mr Yancey, suddenly turning to the tailboard of his lorry. 'Stowaway!' And, eyes glimmering, he pointed into the truck.

No wonder the country air had been alive with grunts, groans and howlings. For there, in a corner, slumped against the old dark sacking, one of his two short legs propped between the iron chain and dingy coils of rope, was Uncle Conway. Shivering and purple-faced — for he was without hat or overcoat — but obviously consoled by his flasks — one already lay emptily on the boards at the tip of the small polished shoe belonging to his other leg — Uncle was behaving much as Mr Mattey had. His eyes were closed, one stumpy arm was dancing through the air, and his lips, though moving, did not always emit words.

'Conway!' gasped Aunt Wells, stricken. 'I — I can't believe it.'

'Wells!' Uncle cried, clutching the side of the truck and struggling half upright. 'Into sanctuary, woman! The shiege. We're starting the shiege.'

'Oh, Mr Mattey,' Aunt cried, distressed. 'What can I say? Oh heavens, the shame!'

Grey hair swinging out from under a wildly angled Homburg, pink bow once more askew, Mr Mattey consulted his silver watch. Then, frowning with both gravity and resolution, he moved lankily, authoritatively, to the tailboard.

'Calm, brother, calm. Inflict no hurt. You have our love, our care.' Sleeves dustily uplifted, stiff white cuffs sliding out, he

133

turned to Mr Yancey. 'Greengage, briskly now. You and I will help this gentleman into the cab. There he may stay. While we worship.'

'Hands shoff!' yelled Uncle Conway, now fully upright. 'This ... ish a Nashionalist lorry. Destinashun ... Madrid!'

'Oh, Conway, please — ' And Aunt Wells, plainly suffering, tried to climb over the tailboard in the wake of Mr Mattey.

'Inside, dear madam. Inside, to your seat and your prayers,' urged Mr Mattey, seizing her arm and pushing her away. The elderly preacher, kneeling on the grubby boards while he recovered breath, looked far more determined than Mr Yancey, who, obviously not relishing the task, still hadn't climbed up. 'God will meet this challenge, never fear.'

'Cow pats,' Uncle shouted, saluting so exuberantly that he almost toppled. 'Bring out the damnashun gums! Fire, I shay, fire!'

'Now,' said Mr Mattey, pulling himself erect, and unable to resist yet another glance at his watch as he did so. 'Shall we establish certain things? Firstly, this is not your truck. You are trespassing, sir. Secondly, we have matters to attend to. God's word cannot wait.'

'Testicles!' raved Uncle Conway, swaying tubbily as he stumbled to the centre of the lorry. 'Out of my way, damn-ed Red! I know you. Jeshus — Jeshus spoke, an called you, shed follow me, follow me, Hall. Ha, ha. An, an you followed. Like — like an old damnashun grey goat!'

'My friend and I,' said Mr Mattey grimly, apparently unaware that the friend was still not with him, 'are going to help you off, into the cab. There, brother, you may sober at your leisure.'

And, stepping forward, he managed to grasp, and hold by the sleeve, Uncle's jaunty arm.

That, unhappily, was the limit of his success. Flapping and struggling to maintain his freedom, small feet pattering like a hail of bullets on the floor of the truck, 'Fire!' Uncle Conway roared to the resplendent if chilly evening. 'Fire, damn it, fire!'

And, with a short, curving, hook-shaped punch, biffed Mr Mattey squarely in the eye. Mr Mattey staggered, but did not fall. It was his watch that fell, striking the boards in a swift doomed flash of silver.

24

The service began. But how could Aunt Wells relax and enjoy worship when, at any instant, there might occur a yell, or fusillade of yells, or even a tipsy personal appearance — Uncle Conway in the doorway, pointing his flask at the faithful as if it were a machine gun! Little wonder Aunt's voice sometimes buckled in mid-verse. Little wonder knees and gloves — soiled a trifle from the tailboard of the truck, as she'd pressed distressed hands to the grimy wood — trembled as she sat and prayed. Little wonder her eyelashes fluttered uncontrollably. Entering the mission from the lane, to the accompaniment of bawdy, triumphant whoopings from Uncle Conway, still bestriding the lorry and defying anyone to get him off, we had encountered a bristlingly sensitive hush. That members of that small congregation had not tiptoed to the door and peered out was hard to believe. What they made of it all was as hidden behind their headstone-rigid faces as was Aunt's turmoil behind her own solemn face. Nodding to the lady with greasy eyebrows who gave out hymn books, and to Mr Raven, the little man with knocking knees, Aunt had sat down in her usual place.

'Concentrate, Gordon. Ignore the tumult outside,' she'd whispered, palely, as I sat beside her. 'Think of other things.'

And, setting me an example, Aunt tremulously crossed hands in the centre of her lap and gazed at Mr Edgar. Playing loudly yet soulfully, as though building a musical escape ladder from earthly strife to heavenly calm, there couldn't have been a better distraction. The little piano tuner's hands flowed and pressed: he coaxed out stops, trailed across the keys with a harpist's grace. Was that how you made babies? I speculated, mind wandering. Were ladies like harps or keyboards, to be strummed upon until they grew fat in the middle? Did Mr Edgar hover over Betty — tuning-fork rapaciously between his teeth — as if she were quivering strings, brushing the tips of his fingers delicately to and fro? Occasionally pausing, here to prod, there to pull? A thumb in her belly button, a finger lingering on her tit hill? Or was there, as the boys at school maintained, something more? But such thoughts were horrible, sacrilegious and uncomfortable! Swiftly I looked away towards the door, just in time to see Mr Mattey's entrance. He looked flushed and puffy; his one eye was half shut. By morning it would be as black as Daniel Damascus.

'Don't worry,' I heard him whisper to Aunt. 'Gallant Greengage is staying with him.' Then, after looking carefully around at the little rows of motionless, studiously averted heads, 'Sidney not here tonight? Praise be.'

'Indeed yes,' Aunt breathed. 'A policeman ... ' Then, as if recollecting her responsibilities, 'Mr Mattey, your watch ...'

'It has stopped,' said Mr Mattey, seeming to shrink inside his clothes as he patted his pocket and leant his chill eyes and face even closer to Aunt's appalled, sympathetic countenance. 'After all these years, the old companion has stopped.'

'There'll be a resurrection, of course,' Aunt Wells said hastily, blinking more rapidly than ever. 'I shall pay for any repairs. In fact, I shall insist upon a new one. A new watch, Mr Mattey. It is the least I can do. After — after what has happened.'

'Please, dear madam — '

Bristly hand in air, Mr Mattey stalked to the front, taking his stance behind the lectern — though not, perhaps, with ease. If the scandal of Charlotte had been a shock, so, in its smaller way, was the loss of his watch — or, at any rate, the loss of its ticking capabilities. Without it his movements seemed painfully, clumsily uncertain. Once, plucking out the injured timepiece, he looked briefly, disbelievingly down at its cherubic countenance before, with a floundering gesture of lean hand, returning it sadly to its pocket.

I was thinking about how babies came — would Betty's, when it came, bounce like a hideously bawling beach ball from behind a pretty yellow towel? — when I looked suddenly up to see Mr Mattey closing the big, family size Bible so thumpingly that dust, spinning madly, rose like a locust swarm to his bad eye. At once water dribbled down to a crescent shaped groove in his grainy cheek, filling the parched pores with a weird glitter. Defiantly tossing back his hair as it flopped like a grey towel drying in the breeze, 'Forgive me, friends,' Mr Mattey said, 'but, with my unhappy eye, reading isn't easy. Better that I should tell you, in my own words, that wonderful story, told so well by St John the divine ... the feeding of the five thousand.'

A kind of haze, like early morning mist rising off the lake of Galilee, seemed to billow around me. For by now I felt almost as if the story were personal to myself, that if I wasn't the youth who bore the basket and palpitatingly grasped it while it filled like a burst dam with loaves and fishes, then I should have been! Back came Mr Mattey's words. 'There is a lad here, a bundle of possibilities. Possibilities for good, possibilities for evil.' And here was I, thinking of bodies and babies, instead of trying to multiply in goodness! 'You are evil, little David. A veritable hob ferret,' I imagined the condemnatory voice of Mr Mattey in a swift lurid daydream. 'I know your thoughts. You are unclean. You have walked a certain rooftop. You have seen Betty Bathsheba at her ablutions. Naughtiness consumes you. You hate Uriah the Edgar, as King David hated Uriah the Hittite.'

'There is a lad here,' intoned Mr Mattey, telling his story, and unfortunately choosing that moment to look directly at me.

Panic! Simmering secret guilt! What was he about to say? Before he exposed me, I must expose him!

Leaping up, knocking askew Mrs Rollins' round grey hat with its look of a worn, fur-coated tongue as that lady sat peaceably nursing her blue veined elbows on the bench in front, 'Stabber!' I yelled, straining every nerve in my throat. 'Stabber of lambs!'

For suddenly I was back in the gunshop by the river. Walking between the tall pillars of stale linoleum. Back among the dowdy old calendars, the tin plate advertisements for a biscuit called Munch, back with the cows in that old oil painting so tipsily hung. Inspired, I saw Mr Mattey in his little glass-walled office. Grey thatch of hair forbiddingly awry, eyes protruding like writhing seaweed as he snatched an open penknife from the table. Lifting it high, cruelly and bloodily slashing it down at an innocent, twisting lamb. Of course! That was why the penknife, lying near the old invoices, the old text cards, had been so moist and red. Mattey killed lambs for sacrifice — just as Abraham had! And the hymns he liked! All about the blood of the Lamb, and dying!

'Stabber! Stabber of lambs!'

The little Bethel, still enjoying cold evening light, seemed to darken a notch as, rocking on my heels, I pointed accusingly at the lectern. The oil lamps, unlit and brassily grinning, looked down on a surge of turned, alarmed heads — the stove in the corner stood rooted in black, well-rounded dismay. Only Mr Edgar did not turn — crouched over his harmonium he continued to survey the keys as if reluctant to lift his gaze from their unvarying tranquillity.

'I've seen the blood!' I shouted. 'And the knife! In his shop. Lamb's blood, like Abraham shed!'

'Sit down, wicked boy!' And Aunt Wells, sickly pale as her pearls, seized my arm, tugging.

'Mattey the murderer!' I yelled, resisting. 'Horrid Hall, the mad knifer!'

One of the two young girls with sticking-out teeth began to giggle, a silvery hysterical rattling. Thwack! Inflamed, her mother slapped her on the knee. Mr Mattey, helpless behind the lectern, seemed divided. The half of him with the good eye dry and stern and shocked, the other half confused and weeping. His hand on the weeping side moved down towards his pocket where the dead watch lay, as if the only thing to be done was to time the interruption, then, recollecting that this in itself was a waste of time, moved back up to dab haplessly, angrily, at the bad eye.

'Arrest him,' I yelled, rallying. 'Put him away! Warm up the condemned cell!'

'Dearie oh dear,' gasped Mrs Rollins, red-cheeked as the feather in her grey hat, eyes blue and bright as the veins on her bare elbows. 'Never known the like. Never! My gooseberries no!'

'Bad!' puffed Mr Marley, the elderly farmer, his pale chins rolling. 'Bad when seed spring up afore its time.'

The hymn book lady, eyebrows glistening darkly with indignation, leant to whisper to Aunt, who nodded tautly.

'Outside, Gordon. This instant.'

'But, Aunt Wells, Mr Mattey thinks he's Abraham. Honest!'

'Outside, Gordon. Do you hear? At *once.*'

'Yes, go, child,' murmured little Mr Raven, gentle forgiving wrinkles around his eyes as he leant, knees knocking, to touch my sleeve. 'Go now. In grace.'

'Disgrace,' I heard Mr Marley mutter as, not altogether reluctantly, I went. 'Bad! Bad harvest!'

25

In the lane I discovered that Uncle Conway was still on the truck, slumped victoriously in his old position beside the iron chain and the dingy coils of rope. As if to make amends for his defeat Mr Greengage Yancey had placed himself self-consciously on guard. He now stood miserably against the tailboard, shoulders hunched, cap low over dripping eyes. A commodious scarf of lurid green had appeared around his scrawny neck. It was the eyes, though, that did it, their abundance of overflowing water triggering off a memory. Of course! Why hadn't I thought of it before? Just like that little man with dripping eyes that Auntie Alex had talked about, Mr Yancey was a woodworm pest! A horror who peered, through draughty holes, at ladies as they undressed in bathing booths! Why else would his eyes be so copiously damp?

'Pest!' I shouted. 'Bare lady pest!'

Mr Yancey leapt in the air, his right elbow striking the truck. His lean neck twisted frenziedly about. From the dirt engrained depths of the lorry, 'Down with Mad-Madrid!' Uncle Conway suddenly clamoured, sounding refreshed and vibrant. 'Up — up Francho!'

And a flask, lobbed through the air, struck Mr Yancey's cap, whizzing it round like a squashed purple carousel.

'Pest!' I repeated enthusiastically. 'Nasty, peeping King David!'

Then, dodging under Mr Yancey's grabbing arm, I crawled on slithering knees to where Uncle sat wagging his small truculent head, open-mouthed and solemn.

'Uncle Conway, Mr Yancey watches ladies undressing at the seaside. He cuts holes in wood to watch them through. Wood!' I shouted vehemently. 'Holes in wood!'

To my disappointment Uncle shook his head, placing an unsteady finger against his mouth.

139

'Thash enuff, Gordon. They'll hear ... inshide. Dishrupt sher-vice.'

Perching on the side of the truck, ignoring the harassed, shivering Mr Yancey, I looked thoughtfully down at Uncle's gently wagging head.

'You're drunk, aren't you, Uncle Conway? You're a disgrace. Like me.'

This Uncle carefully digested, before frowning contentiously.

'Wanna ... wanna be deshired,' he said at last, painfully. 'Wanna — be — loved.'

'Aunt Wells loves you, Uncle Conway.'

'Yesh, boy, but afterwards ... she never talks about it. Thash bad. A bad shign.'

'After what, Uncle Conway?'

Instead of answering Uncle Conway fumblingly picked up his remaining flask, tipped it upside down, and watched in despair as only a drop of pale liquid toppled out.

'Uncle Conway, do *you* think Auntie Alex is going to die?'

'Alex? Shilly woman. Shilly women don't die.'

'You gave her the house, didn't you, Uncle Conway? The house with the balcony, and the blue shutters, and the general inside one of the rooms on his white horse. You took it from the loft and gave it her. You see, I know. I listened behind the door with Aunt Wells. That's how Aunt Wells knew. I didn't tell her about the little house. Honest. You said if I didn't tell her I could have a camera.'

Uncle Conway nodded several times, each nod more drunkenly profound than the last. Mr Yancey, having turned his back on us, was now staring with huddled concentration at the sky. Now that the sun was gone the heavens were turning into a replica of his own cloth cap, bulging and heavy with a lowering peak.

'Was Auntie Alex very pleased with the house, Uncle Conway? Did she give you a kiss?'

'She gave me a glash, Gordon, and thash all. Sherry ... sherry wine.'

'What else did you want, Uncle Conway?'

'Nothing!' Uncle rapped, sounding suddenly sober. 'Nothing! But, damn it, it's shnice to be offered!' And, petulantly, he hurled the flask to a corner where, battered and rejected, it stood shuddering against the walls of the truck.

The journey back couldn't have been quieter. Aunt Wells had stalked from the mission drawn and cold, as if, for once, untouched by the warmth of worship. With a tired curt nod she had accepted Mr Yancey's helping hand into the cab. Weary by now of Uncle's morose, muttering company, as well as being cold myself, I'd joined her on the long leather seat where, instinctively, she'd taken my hand before, abruptly, letting go of it. When Mr Mattey joined us he gave me a typical look of fierce, bleak humour. 'This young boy does not appear to know the truth of what he sees. That I was not committing the sacrificial lamb for slaughter, but had been cutting up meat for Caesar!'

'Cutting up meat? For Caesar. Mr — Mr Yancey's dog?'

'Yes, Caesar was my charge that day. What have you to say to that, young Adam?'

'Well, Gordon, what have you to say to Mr Mattey?' Aunt asked me, in a voice as chill as the evening air. 'No, Mr Yancey, pray do not start your estimable truck. I wish to hear every word that the boy has to utter. If it does not satisfy me then out in the lane he goes. Others, perhaps, will be so foolish as to take him in and rear him.'

'Sorry, Mr Mattey,' I mumbled at last. 'It — it wasn't a lamb, was it? It was dog's meat you were cutting up. Meat for Caesar. Not — not meat for Jehovah!'

'Render unto Caesar, eh, young ferret?' Mr Mattey said, with a touch of the old, watch-in-hand lightness. 'Render unto Caesar. Excellent! Excellent! I shall remember that. Long after tonight. Long after my eye has healed!'

When the truck at last reached our drive and stopped we all got slowly, stiffly out. Mr Yancey's blue eyes were swimming with cold, the green scarf had crept up to his newly shining nostrils. The two men, first Mr Yancey, then Mr Mattey with a quick reassuring clasp, shook Aunt's hand under the grey, still trees, then Aunt turned silently, unhappily towards the house. It was Mr Yancey, looking over his tailboard into the truck, who gave the alarm.

'Goshums! Where's the guv?'

The space between rope and chain was startlingly, blatantly empty. Uncle Conway was gone.

26

The evening grew uneasily older. I wasn't even sent to bed. Sam and Mrs Hampton, of course, were in their own homes; there was only Aunt's anxious flittering and my own nervous padding from room to room — as if I might suddenly come across Uncle lurking in jocular playfulness, squashed down with a bottle, and a small raucous song, in some odd corner. For a while, with an effort of will, Aunt settled at a table, staring down at her thin, firmly pressed hands — the colourless nails cut in perfect crescents of utter cleanliness, the skin taut, almost translucent. (Those hands — had impatience with Uncle Conway made them too perfunctory? Did they hold a hymn book, dust a vase or alter the hands of a clock more considerately than their attention to a husband? Had they cossetted enough, had they loved enough? Aunt must have wondered.)

The corridors and rooms grew dim, curtains swished and lights came on. Now Aunt walked about again; somehow thinner than her twin set, slighter than her tweed skirt. Inappropriate to be dressed so rumbustiously, so practically, for she was all spirit now as even I could see — all spirit and icy self-reproach. For had she done enough? Had she done anything — except flee inside the mission, hope people wouldn't notice what was going on. And for what? To protect the sensibilities of the faithful? To protect their *pride*? And especially hers. Oh pride was surely not the business of it all, what mattered was loving — not adhering to formulae, a ritual of prayers and hymns. For what use sermons when a house called Welcome was barred against its enemy, when a man stood guard and kept that enemy at bay?

'Yet, I wonder,' Aunt said aloud, obviously tormented. 'Can the cities of the righteous open their gates? Won't the enemy swallow them? Take their charity? Corrupt them? Musn't every house put up its shutters, barricade its doors? Be busy within itself. Hugging its own faith while, outside, the devil rages?'

'Houses don't hug, Aunt Wells,' I said, puzzled. 'They haven't arms.'

But Aunt was silent again. Did every Bethel end like this — a fortress, a city closed against the infidel?

It was ten o'clock by the most punctilious and statesmanlike of our clocks, the tall one with an infinity of hair-thin scratchings all across its seedy yellow face, when the front door thundered martially. 'Oh dear,' said Aunt Wells, pausing in her stride, looking quickly at me. It was just like that time in the hall with Aunt and I eavesdropping, the two of us bound together, now as then, by mutual alarm. Her hands looked cold, and I knew that my knees were — cold as the attic high above us, or the garage loft outside. (Surely a cheerless world tonight, that loft, with only the cocoons, the muslin wastelands spun by spiders, to keep one warm?)

Turning, Aunt Wells went to answer the door. Presently voices — Aunt's and a deeper voice — the sound of the front door closing, the sound of trudging, squeaking feet across our hall, over our carpets. A belated clock chiming quickly in as though protesting, and then in came Aunt, her paleness more tightly drawn than ever. Looking at me with eyes that lived in deepening hollows, Aunt said, 'Gordon, this is Sergeant Rushkin. You remember?' A tremble in her voice.

'Now, madam, no real need to distress yourself,' the sergeant said, an edifice of both gloom and comfort, buttons shining, helmet and gloves awkwardly between large, sandy haired hands until — perhaps to ease the atmosphere — the two articles of office were placed formally on our table. 'Not murder to be drunk and disorderly, though the way some folk carry on you'd think it was. Mind you, madam, you won't get him back till morning. Too aggressive by half, my word yes. Must have been round half the pubs in town. Talk about a human drain pipe!'

'Conway in a prison cell,' Aunt Wells said. 'It's insufferable, Sergeant Rushkin.' She seemed unable to take her gaze from the table, from the objects of the law next to the flower vase on the burnished wood.

'Station cell,' corrected the sergeant. 'Not as simple as that though, is it?'

Aunt Wells sat down beside me at the table. She took my hand, and waited.

'Took, purloined that is, the horse from the corner field, the gentleman did. The old white horse that's always there. Took it and marched it bold as brass into Mrs Hallet's place, of which he seems uncommonly fond. That's where our constable spotted him. In her garden. Embracing the horse and,' here Sergeant Rushkin paused to look away and cough discreetly behind a big homely wedge of raw-knuckled hand, 'bellowing to be let in at the front door. Yelling about a general or something. Lucky the place was empty — given the lady a fatal fit if she'd still been there. By the way, madam,' another cough behind the same vast hand. 'how is the lady? Very popular she was. Tough and jolly. Quite the queen of the York Arms.'

'The horse,' Aunt Wells said stiffly. 'It wasn't —'

'No, the quadruped's quite unharmed, madam. No need to fret on that score. Funny thing for him to do though, all the same.'

'I bet he wasn't bareback on her,' I couldn't help interjecting. 'Dolly would have tossed him off!'

'Now, Gordon.' But Aunt was too upset to sound angry. Was she going to cry? To weep before the sergeant? Inwardly shrinking in shame at such a horrifying thought I moved nearer Aunt as if to remind her, by scraping chair legs, to be hard and strong. But Aunt didn't cry though there were a few stately blinks. Of what was she thinking now behind that shuttered, tired face? That Uncle Conway was so impossible he ought to be left in the police station for ever? That no man who loved her, even slightly, could behave as he behaved? And always would behave? Was there really no escape from being the injured, humiliated queen of the big quiet house of ancient clocks, ornate old carpets?

'You were asking about Mrs Hallet,' Aunt Wells said at last. 'She is recovering. Or so her son-in-law, whom I saw earlier this evening, informs me. And now, Sergeant Rushkin, a cup of cocoa to help you keep out the cold? Or perhaps,' Aunt's voice trailed a little, as if hoping for refusal, for a heartening rejection of even a mild part of that modest store of alcohol — the official store, that is, not counting Uncle's numerous flasks and bottles — which the old house dutifully kept, 'a small glass of green ginger wine?'

27

By morning the snow had come. (As Sam, arriving reluctantly for work, growlingly put it, 'The dragon's a-snapping. A-showing his pearly whites.') It lay everywhere, on the slope of the garage roof, along the garden paths, under the trees of the drive. It lay, shining, across the summerhouse. It lay, furled and virginal, along the stretch of garden wall shared by us with Belle Lilac. And with the snow, curiously, a lightening of Aunt Wells' spirits. As if the unseasonable sparkle outside brought tingling courage, a refreshment to her sorely tried soul. 'Gordon,' she said, quite brightly, before packing me off to school after a breakfast during which Mrs Hampton's frequent probings as to Uncle Conway's whereabouts had been stoically endured, 'Gordon, no school for you this afternoon. You will hand this note to Mr Flood. And please return promptly for lunch.'

When I got home again — not promptly as Aunt had asked, but lamentably late — she was sitting alone at the dining room table. After placing before me a large steaming plate of haddock, mashed potatoes and parsley sauce, she sat, head inclined, as though saying grace.

'What are you thanking Jehovah for this time, Aunt Wells? Not for the pepper, because the pot's empty. Or it isn't coming out because the holes are all bunged up.'

'I was thanking God, Gordon, for new opportunities, for new strength. The strength to keep on. The strength not to resign from life. Or, for that matter, resign from anything.'

Wrinkling my nose in the steam from the yellow grey shadings of the haddock, I was silent for a moment. Aunt had sounded very serious.

'Where's Uncle Conway?' I said at last. 'Still in prison? Oh Aunt Wells, will *he* have the strength? To escape? Before they put him in the electric chair? Or make him swing from a rope till his neck breaks off!'

'He's upstairs, Gordon, having a bath. The first thing I insisted

145

on when he arrived home. I've already given his suit to Sam to give to his brother-in-law. It was quite unretainable after that ... last night. Grained and dirty from the lorry, and splashed beyond forbearance.'

'Aunt Wells, why aren't I going to school this afternoon? What are we going to do?'

For the first time Aunt Wells looked a little less than equable. Appetite deserting her, she put down her knife and fork.

'We are going, Gordon, to act as neighbours should. We are going to the infirmary.'

Dropping my fork in dissent I cried out, terrified.

'We're going as a family. All three of us. Your Uncle agrees that this is the proper course. There's nothing to fear. Your ... Betty's mother is recovering speedily, I am glad to say. So, when you've finished eating, you will go and wash and change to your best suit. No, Gordon, you will not stay behind to help Sam clear the snow — it is already clearing itself. Please, no nonsense! I have had a trying time.' She paused, head slightly curved, a drooping of sorrow enlivened by the last frail wisps of rising steam from her forgotten haddock. 'Really, it has been a quite impossible spring. I don't think that any of us has behaved quite normally.'

The infirmary, a huddled downcast grey and brown old building, stood across the road that ran along one side of the park. The park itself was now a patchwork, with the green looking particularly rich and fresh and the white discoloured. We walked in the Maytime sunshine through the park, Aunt tall and quiet under a spiritedly lighthearted, monumental hat of powdery blue, with dustings on her cheeks as delicate as the bloom on the grapes in a bag she carried, Uncle subdued and bundled under his brushed black bowler, the black buttons of his overcoat in the clear flashing light as tired and sombre as his eyes. In his hand he carried flowers. Limply I trailed behind, scuffling my feet, desperate, hoping still for escape. Thinking of everything that I didn't want to think of. Owls and mice, the commode with the pretty raspberry coloured cushion, the floodtide of woolly, allegedly insanitary rabbits once owned by Miss Young and Miss Cuthbert, the long lordly lonely path to Belle Lilac. Of the mermaid and her bold little breasts, of Betty in the tiny yellow towel — Passing the park bandstand I saw a girl, possibly a year or two older than myself — why wasn't *she* at school, had she a

146

cold? leaning excitedly over the rail, swinging over as far as she dared. When she saw me she pointed down at the grass. 'I've dropped my sweet. Please. Will you pick it up? It's only half sucked.' I actually saw the toffee on the ground, twisted and brown and shining from her mouth as it lay amid the tiny melting glaciers of the park. Ignoring it, and her, I went on walking. I felt, suddenly, positively and wretchedly sick.

I remember the infirmary as a place of benches, of stern paint washed walls as palely green as the sea, and of corridors that seemed to go on and on like train tunnels.

'Sister says that you may come in with us for a few minutes,' Aunt Wells told me. 'Here, you may give the grapes.' Into my hands she pushed the brown paper bag of black round fruit.

The room was small and narrow with a strong antiseptic odour and white sheets. The silvery steel frame of the bed had a cold cathedral sanctity. The afternoon sun, now only vaguely realised (oh how I missed its warmth) was still out in the park. Somewhere over the damp infirmary rooftops, the slates of which sloped darkly down almost to bump the small dingy window. Auntie Alex, I saw, was sitting up in bed in a rosy nightdress with fancy trimming all the way down the open floating neckline. She looked like one of her fat pink slippers, her face the fluffy white tassel, drained and nodding as she summoned strength. Aunt's hand, on my shoulder, pushed me forward; holding the bag of grapes I stood gazing into the widow's face — bleaker than formerly with only moderate make-up, but the indefatigably red mouth looked almost normal, just slightly bent perhaps, but really no more than a pulled-down tremble, a forlorn tug of full and garish corner lip.

'Grapes,' I said, avoiding her eyes. 'For you, Auntie Alex. To make you better.'

She reached out, seizing my arm. Now I was frighteningly near her. Breathing her breath, feeling the strange cupboardy warmth from her body. Still clutching me, she pulled my ear round to where her mouth was.

'Best in the world, aren't they, son? Aren't they, little Franco?' I heard her whisper, with only the slightest faltering of depleted voice, her mouth tight as a ventriloquist's as she breathed down my ear. 'Biggest and best. Like them big stone ones by the Nile. Them pyramids.'

I knew what she meant.

147

'They're the best in the world, Auntie Alex,' I whispered back. 'Really they are. Better than the pyramids. Honest!'

She let go of me then, already grinning crookedly past me at Aunt Wells and Uncle Conway.

'My God, good of you all, I must say. Grapes and flowers. Oh my God! Just like in the old days. With — with Betty slap-banging inside me, and my good late Noel — God bless him! bringing me comforts. Olive oil and treacle, that's what I craved in them days.' She paused, catching her breath. 'Enough — enough to make any baby — begging pardon, Wells, for my indelicate — slide out premature on its little red rug!'

Outside, alone in the long corridor, I sat down on a bench to wait. Released by Aunt Wells from the bondage of the sick room I felt exhilarated, happy beyond belief. Good old Auntie! Why, not only should I have given her the grapes, but also the little book of love poems that I'd rescued from the dustbin. That would really have made me her favourite again. That would really have ensured that my imaginary little mouse would be forgotten.

I looked up. Betty was standing beside me, looking down. She seemed different in her thickish winter coat, maybe a little thicker herself — I wasn't sure. But different she was.

'Well now, Gordon,' she said, bitingly, 'guess what I've found out! Though mother, bless her, didn't even want to tell me. But she did, and now I know exactly what a helpful little man you turned out to be! Leaving her, as you did, on the floor and saying nothing! Do you understand that she might have *died!* Do you understand, do you even begin to understand, what a terrible thing you did, you wicked boy?'

'There — there was a mouse,' I began, then stopped. But she wasn't talking about mice. Or mermaids. Only about my leaving Auntie Alex on the floor!

'I don't think that I ever want to see you again,' Betty said, turning away. 'I honestly didn't think a boy could be so callous. Or so stupid. Please, in future, keep out of my sight! Mother may forgive you but I, I never shall!'

After she had gone, presumably into the sick room, and before Aunt Wells and Uncle Conway came out to join me, I took from my coat pocket the little red rattle (yes, a baby's rattle, and oh the shame of getting it, the blushes!) bought that morning on my way home from school with the shilling that Mr Edgar had given me, the rattle that was intended as a present for Betty's baby when

148

it came, and, bending, shoved it frantically out of view under the seat. A strange defeated little oddment for the infirmary cleaning ladies to find when next they came to clean, their pails clattering, their mops dropping and thudding like bombs on some far off city.